## She watched Brady run his fingers over the surface of the rock slabs

An unexpected warmth flowed along Audrey's arms at the thought of those long fingers doing the same thing to her skin. Maybe she had stayed in the sun too long that morning and baked her brain.

She felt as if she was experiencing Brady overload. She'd caught herself snatching glimpses of him ever since they'd arrived at the store, glimpses she didn't dare make in the car because he would have noticed.

Each time she looked at him, the more attractive he became.

The archetypal sexy carpenter. She wondered if he looked as good as she imagined in nothing but a pair of jeans and a tool belt.

But she couldn't risk getting too involved, not when it could put everything she had and was trying to build at risk.

Dear Reader,

I'm excited to share my second Harlequin American Romance novel, *Her Very Own Family*, with you. The backdrop of the story is a place familiar to me—the gorgeous northeast corner of Tennessee. The area is verdant, mountainous and filled with soothing creeks and rushing rivers.

The beauty and calm of the setting are just what Audrey York needs when she arrives in tiny Willow Glen. Audrey came to life while I was pondering how someone would respond if she were caught up in a scandal not of her making. How could she start over when the scandal made national news? Could she escape the guilty-by-association way people looked at her and find a man to see and love the real her?

This book is the result of all that pondering, and it is Audrey's journey to letting go, trusting, forgiving and finding love with a hunky carpenter named Brady Witt, who has his own past to overcome on the road to love.

I hope you enjoy Audrey and Brady's story. I'd love to hear what you think. You can e-mail me through my Web site at www.trishmilburn.com.

Happy reading!

*Trish Milburn*

# Her Very Own Family
## TRISH MILBURN

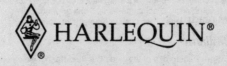

HARLEQUIN®

TORONTO • NEW YORK • LONDON
AMSTERDAM • PARIS • SYDNEY • HAMBURG
STOCKHOLM • ATHENS • TOKYO • MILAN • MADRID
PRAGUE • WARSAW • BUDAPEST • AUCKLAND

Recycling programs
for this product may
not exist in your area.

ISBN-13: 978-0-373-75264-5
ISBN-10:    0-373-75264-4

HER VERY OWN FAMILY

Copyright © 2009 by Trish Milburn.

All rights reserved. Except for use in any review, the reproduction or
utilization of this work in whole or in part in any form by any electronic,
mechanical or other means, now known or hereafter invented, including
xerography, photocopying and recording, or in any information storage
or retrieval system, is forbidden without the written permission of the
publisher, Harlequin Enterprises Limited, 225 Duncan Mill Road,
Don Mills, Ontario M3B 3K9, Canada.

This is a work of fiction. Names, characters, places and incidents are
either the product of the author's imagination or are used fictitiously,
and any resemblance to actual persons, living or dead, business
establishments, events or locales is entirely coincidental.

This edition published by arrangement with Harlequin Books S.A.

® and TM are trademarks of the publisher. Trademarks indicated with
® are registered in the United States Patent and Trademark Office, the
Canadian Trade Marks Office and in other countries.

www.eHarlequin.com

Printed in U.S.A.

## ABOUT THE AUTHOR

Trish Milburn wrote her first book in the fifth grade and has the cardboard-and-fabric-bound handwritten and colored-pencil-illustrated copy to prove it. That "book" was called *Land of the Misty Gems*, and not surprisingly it was a romance. She's always loved stories with happy endings, whether those stories come in the form of books, movies, TV programs or marriage to her own hero.

A print journalist by trade, she still does contract and freelance work in that field, balancing those duties with her dream-come-true career as a novelist. Before she published her first book, she was an eight-time finalist in the prestigious Golden Heart contest sponsored by Romance Writers of America, winning twice. Other than reading, Trish enjoys traveling (by car or train—she's a terra firma girl!), watching TV and movies, hiking, nature photography and visiting national parks.

You can visit Trish online at www.trishmilburn.com. Readers also can write to her at P.O. Box 140875, Nashville, TN 37214-0875.

### Books by Trish Milburn

**HARLEQUIN AMERICAN ROMANCE**
1228—A FIREFIGHTER IN THE FAMILY

To Shane,
who has been my own real-life hero for nineteen years.

And to Jennifer and Jeanie. Thanks for introducing me
to the world of romance fiction way back when.

Writing groups and friends mean a lot to a writer,
and I'm very fortunate to have great wealth
in this area. Although I can't name everyone,
I want to thank three groups in particular for their
unceasing support and wonderful friendship.
Here's to you, Music City Romance Writers,
Wet Noodle Posse and Romance Bandits.

Finally, huge thanks again to the ladies
who are my partners in my career—
my fabulous agent, Michelle Grajkowski;
my wonderful editor, Johanna Raisanen;
and senior editor extraordinaire, Kathleen Scheibling.

## Chapter One

Audrey York scanned the grocery's shelves, familiarizing herself with the offerings. While they were more limited than what she was used to, that was actually okay with her.

She wheeled her cart into the next aisle and nearly collided with an older man who was staring at the shelf in front of him with what could only be called frantic confusion.

"Which one is it?" he mumbled. "There are so many." He reached for one kind of cherry pie filling, then another, then back to the original before dropping his hand in defeat.

"Can I help you?"

He jumped as if he hadn't noticed her or the rattling cart containing her groceries. His eyes, which looked on the verge of tears, glanced from her to the shelf then back to her.

"I don't know which one to get. My wife always buys the groceries."

Poor guy. He was clearly out of his comfort zone. She examined the choices. The Glen Grocery might not carry fresh herbs, but it did offer half a dozen types of cherry pie filling.

"What is it for, pie or cobbler?"

"Cobbler. Her cobbler's the best."

Audrey smiled then picked up a can. "Then I'd suggest this one."

He accepted the can as if it were the Holy Grail. "Thank you." He placed it in the cart alongside a package of chicken thighs, a bag of potatoes, another of flour and a loaf of plain white bread.

Audrey watched him as he moved on up the aisle, something about the helplessness in his eyes tearing at her heart. She fought the urge to give him a hand with the remainder of his grocery shopping. Instead, she continued with her own, sticking to necessities to keep her final bill as low as possible. She didn't *need* the fudge-covered Oreos anyway.

By the time she finished her tour of the rest of the store and headed to the cash register with her purchases, the older man was exiting the front door. As she began piling her items on the conveyor belt, she noticed the checker watching the man with a sad expression on her face. She shook her head and echoed the "poor guy" sentiment Audrey had thought a few minutes before.

"He seemed a little lost," she said to the young woman whose short, choppy magenta hair seemed out of place in quaint little Willow Glen. A quick glance at her name tag revealed her identity as Meg.

"He is," Meg said. "He and his wife were married for more than forty years."

His sadness suddenly made sense. "She died?"

"Yeah, about a month ago. He had family visiting for a while afterward, but now he's alone. I think this is his first trip to the store by himself."

Tears stung Audrey's eyes. She looked toward the ceiling to close off her tear ducts, a trick she'd learned from her mother.

"That'll be $53.76," Meg said, dragging Audrey back to the present.

After paying and placing all her bags in her cart, Audrey headed outside, hoping the bright spring sunshine would burn away the sorrow she'd felt for the older man.

She stuffed the groceries in the trunk of her Jetta, forcing her mind to focus on the endless list of tasks waiting for her when she got home. She liked staying busy even if she had given up a faster-paced life in Nashville for a more soul-nurturing existence in the mountains of East Tennessee.

As she started for the driver's-side door, she noticed the older man again. When he wiped his cheek, it tugged at her emotions. She wanted to help him, but what good could she do? Bringing back his wife wasn't possible, and most people hated pity from others. Not to mention she was still wary about meeting new people, something she'd have to get past if she wanted to make a success of her new life here.

Still, she found herself walking across the parking lot

toward him, hoping she'd come up with something to say by the time she reached his side.

"Excuse me," she said as she came within a few feet of him. "I'm sorry to bother you, but I was wondering if you could help me."

The man made one more quick swipe at his right eye before facing her.

"I'm new to Willow Glen, and I was wondering if you could tell me if there is anywhere nearby where I could get some nice picture frames, bigger ones." She held her hands about two feet apart.

"There's a Wal-Mart down in Elizabethton."

She shook her head but kept a smile firmly in place. "I was hoping for something a bit more unique, hand-crafted if at all possible." She was a long way from needing the frames for her wildflower photos yet, but it was the first thing that had tumbled out of her mouth. And it proved a nice, neutral topic.

"Well, I've fiddled with a few here and there, though I mainly make furniture now."

"Really? Then it's my lucky day." She extended her hand. "I'm Audrey York. I'm fixing up the old Grayson Mill, turning it into a café."

"Nelson Witt. Nice to meet you." He shook her hand, the calluses on his weathered palm revealing he did indeed work with his hands. "The old mill, huh? That'll probably take a lot of work."

She laughed. "You're right there. I think I've already swept out enough dirt to create a new county." Her mood lifted when she saw a hint of a smile on Mr. Witt's gray-stubbled face. Despite everything that had happened in the past year to sour her outlook, it still felt good and natural to help people, to bring some happiness into their lives.

"Guess I could put together some frames and bring them out there sometime."

"That would be great."

"When would be good for you?"

Audrey detected how he leaped on the opportunity, probably looking for anything to keep his mind off the absence of his other half. "I'm there pretty much all the time except when I'm running errands."

"You staying out there?"

"Yeah. I'm turning the loft into my living area, and the bottom level will house the café."

"I'd say something about wondering if that was safe, but I know you young people think yourselves invincible."

"Considering I've lived in the city and been flying across the continent nearly every week for the past five years, this feels as safe as Mayberry."

"Well, then, when I finish the frames, I'll run them by."

"Thank you."

After a couple more minutes of talking, Audrey headed back to her car, her heart lighter. She'd probably had no more than five minutes of conversation with Mr. Witt, but she already really liked him. And if she could help ease a little of his pain, then it was a good day.

Not to mention she yearned for new friends here, craved them. The past year had left a yawning, dark hole in her life, and she couldn't wait to fill it.

AUDREY SPENT the rest of the morning cleaning, burning useless debris and adding to her list of needed supplies while trying not to think about how much those supplies would cost. When she stopped long enough to fix a late lunch of grilled chicken and pasta salad from the grocery's deli, she heard gravel popping on the lane leading back to the gristmill.

She stepped out onto the small porch attached to the front of the mill. Eventually, it would be the attractive entrance to her café, but now only a cheap folding lawn chair and an upturned five-gallon bucket she used for a table occupied the space. She shaded her eyes against the sun and saw Mr. Witt stepping out of his truck.

"That was fast." She smiled wide, happy to see this potential friend so soon.

Mr. Witt shrugged. "They don't take long to make. Thought I'd whip together some samples, see if you like them," he said as he lowered the tailgate of his pickup.

When she saw the size of the wooden crate he pulled toward the back of the truck, she hurried to help him. "Here, I'll get this side. I'm not much for watching other people do my work." She added the last, hoping to forestall any argument that he was still capable of carrying a heavy box. She figured he'd had enough reminding today that things weren't as they'd always been.

Audrey backed her way toward the mill, Mr. Witt following. Once inside, she guided the crate onto the bench stretching along the length of one wall.

"I haven't been in here in years," Mr. Witt said as he

scanned the interior. "I remember coming here with my daddy when I was a boy."

"Really?"

"Oh, yeah. Even though you could get cornmeal in the stores, he always liked what came from the mill better. I remember sitting on the creek bank, just watching the wheel turn round and round."

"That's one of the things on my extensive to-do list," Audrey said. "I want to get the wheel operational again. I think it'll add to the atmosphere."

Mr. Witt looked around at the mill's silent gears and aging wood. "Hard to imagine this place as a restaurant."

"I admit, it's got a long way to go. But as it happens, you're my first dining guest." She extended her arm to point out the small table in the corner, covered with a white cloth and with a vase of daffodils. Her attempt to add a little cheer to the place. "I was about to have lunch, and I've got plenty to share."

"I don't want you to go to all that trouble."

"It's no trouble. I have to eat anyway, and it's the least I can do for you bringing these frames all the way over here." Plus, if Mrs. Witt had always done the grocery shopping, chances were she'd also done the cooking. That led Audrey to believe Mr. Witt might not have been eating properly since his family's departure. Something about him brought out her protective instincts.

"It's not too far," he said as he took a seat. "I just live a couple miles down the road from your lane."

Audrey slid onto the chair opposite him. "Oh, so we're practically neighbors."

Mr. Witt shared tales of his youth in Willow Glen as they ate their lunch, making Audrey laugh with the accounts of some of his mischievous antics.

"I think by the time I got out of school, the teachers were ready to throw a party."

"I can't imagine why. Doesn't everyone bring snakes to show-and-tell and put scarecrows in their teachers' cars?"

Mr. Witt chuckled at the remembered scenes. "But, Lordy, I got payback when I had my own son."

"Wild one, huh?"

"Whoo-ee. Put me to shame. But he turned out all right, so I guess no harm came of his escapades."

"You only have the one?"

"Yeah, just one son. Betty…" Sadness drifted across his face at the name. "Betty and I had two children. Brady's the oldest. He runs the construction company now, even opened a new office where he lives down in Kingsport. Our daughter, Sophie, owns a bridal shop in Asheville, North Carolina. She's got two little girls who I've been known to spoil from time to time."

"I bet you do." Audrey smiled, glad the topic of his grandchildren had pushed away the incredible ache it was painful to witness.

"Does your son have children?"

"Goodness, no. That boy doesn't slow down long enough to date a gal for more than a month at a time. Say, maybe I should fix the two of you up. You're a pretty girl, hardworking."

Audrey wadded her napkin into a ball and tossed it

onto her empty plate. She tried to push away an ache of her own by changing the subject. "I think my only dates are going to be with a broom and a paintbrush for the foreseeable future."

"All work and no play…" he teased.

"Opens my café and adds to my dwindling bank account sooner." She took a drink of her water.

"He's a good-looking boy." The hopeful tone in his voice nearly made Audrey chuckle.

"Must take after his father." She patted his hand. "Let's take a look at those frames." And steer clear of the topic of dating. She didn't have the time or the inclination.

Yes, she got lonely and missed being held. But Darren, the man she'd thought she'd marry, had shown her that might never be possible.

Not when any interesting, or interested, man found out who she was.

BRADY WITT HUNG UP the phone in his office, trying not to worry that he couldn't reach his dad. He'd made attempts all day with no luck. Maybe his dad was out in his shop. Though with the way Nelson had been acting when Brady left, he couldn't imagine it. With his wife's death, the life had seemed to go out of Nelson Witt, too.

"You okay?"

Brady looked up to see his business partner and best friend, Craig Williams, standing in the doorway.

"Yeah, just can't get in touch with Dad."

"He could've gone into town."

"Maybe, but I've been calling all day. If he hit every

business in Willow Glen, it might take him a couple of hours. And that's if he spent an hour hanging out with the other old coots at Cora's Coffee Shop."

Craig ambled in and sank into one of the chairs opposite Brady's desk. "Why don't you take some time off? Go spend it with your dad."

"I just did that."

Craig shook his head. "You were dealing with the funeral and the aftermath. I'm thinking you go up and keep him busy, take him fishing, get him in a new routine that won't remind him of your mom so much."

Brady leaned back in his chair and sighed. "I don't think he's interested in fishing or anything else for that matter."

"Your parents were so close. That's why you should go. Left to themselves, sometimes older people don't last long if they lose their spouse. I saw it happen to my grandma."

The thought of losing his father so soon after his mom sent a sharp pain through Brady's chest. But how did you force someone to learn to live again?

"Just a couple of weeks," Craig said. "We've got things under control here. And if you still feel like you can't do anything after that, then you come back and let time do its thing."

Brady glanced at the calendar. "I've got to finish the bid on the Lakeview project."

"I can finish it up, get Kelly to help me. Be good experience for her. Plus, it's not like you're headed to the wilds of Tibet."

Brady considered Craig's words for a moment before nodding. "Okay." It did make sense to give Kelly, their architecture intern, experience in all aspects of the business.

And honestly, Brady's heart wasn't in his work anyway. He couldn't turn off the anger or pain about his mom's death. Or the concern about how suddenly old and empty his father had looked in the days after the passing of the love of his life.

Maybe time alone with his dad would do Brady some good, too.

For the hour it took him to drive to Willow Glen, he tossed around ideas in his head, things to do with his dad. Fishing, going to visit Sophie and her family, yard work, watching some baseball, maybe even some renovation on the house.

When he pulled into his dad's driveway, he noticed the truck wasn't there. He hadn't seen the truck in town or in the parking lot of Witt Construction's main office. It was after five. Where could his dad be?

Even though he knew he wouldn't find him, Brady did a walk-through of the shop and the house. He'd been in the house while his parents were away from home hundreds of times, but today felt different, emptier. He half expected to step into the kitchen to see his mom at the stove making dinner, an apron tied around her waist and her cheeks pink from the heat. But the kitchen proved even quieter than the rest of the house. His heart ached to know his mom would never again playfully smack his hand away from whatever she was cooking.

He left the lingering presence of his mother behind and stepped out onto the porch.

However this trip turned out, he was getting his dad a cell phone and teaching him how to use it.

"You looking for your dad?"

Brady glanced to his left to see Bernie Stoltz, his parents' longtime neighbor, in his garden.

"Yeah, I've been trying to reach him all day."

"He's probably still out at the old Grayson Mill. He's been spending a lot of time out there with the lady who bought it."

Shock squeezed the air from Brady's lungs. His mother had been gone barely a month. Who was this woman attracting his dad's attention? What did she want from him?

He tried to keep the suspicion out of his voice when he spoke, though. "Someone bought the old mill?"

Bernie leaned on his hoe. "Yep. I hear she's planning to turn it into a restaurant."

Brady had a million more questions, but he'd save them for his father. Bernie was a nice guy, but he tended to be a bit gossipy. And despite Willow Glen's laid-back atmosphere, one thing that had supersonic speed was the gossip chain. Not much else to do in a one-stoplight town.

"Interesting. Well, I guess I'll run out there and see if I can catch him."

He waved to Bernie as he headed for his truck, not inviting further conversation. On his way to the mill, he tried not to jump to conclusions, but he knew how quickly some women leaped on newly widowed men, especially ones with money. His surging suspicions brought an image of Ginny Carter to the surface, but he flung it away with a growl.

At the very least something was odd. Only a few days ago, his dad had been walking around in a daze, weighed down by grief. Now he was spending his free time with some unnamed woman at a run-down gristmill.

When he drove within view of the old building, sure enough, there was his dad's truck under the shade of a big sycamore tree. He rolled to a stop and caught sight of his dad poking his head out the front door of the mill. By the time he stepped out of the truck, his dad stood on the small porch.

"Didn't expect to see you," his dad said.

"I've been calling you all day."

Nelson Witt's gray eyebrows raised. "So you drove all the way up here to check on me?"

"Partly. Decided to take a couple weeks of vacation."

He saw his dad frown. "I suppose Bernie told you where I was," Nelson said, almost his old self again.

"Yeah. He said you've been spending a lot of time out here."

"It passes the days."

There might be hints of his dad's normal self resurfacing, but it was going to be a long time, if ever, before the soul-deep sorrow went away.

"So, you're helping the lady with a little work?" Brady nodded at the wood chips and dust coating his dad's shirt and jeans.

"Yeah, doing some odds and ends now, but she's

going to have me make the tables and chairs for the restaurant eventually."

Brady eyed the exterior of the old mill. "She really thinks people will come out here to eat?"

"They'll come. Audrey's smart, got a business plan, lots of great ideas."

Brady didn't know what he thought of his father's glowing report. On the one hand, it was great that he had a project, something to keep him occupied. On the other, well, he just needed to meet this Audrey for himself to make sure nothing was fishy, that she wasn't a gold digger looking for someone to bankroll her pet project.

"She around?"

His dad nodded toward the gravel lane leading back to the main road. "She's gone into town to get some paint. Should be back soon."

"Well, let's see what you're working on," Brady said as he walked toward the porch.

His dad showed him the benches extending along one wall that he'd reinforced. The railing he'd built around the mill's large gears to keep anyone from stepping too close and getting hurt. And how he was cutting out a section of wall next to the waterwheel so that a large window could be installed, affording a view of the wheel and the creek beyond.

"Sounds like Audrey's kept you busy. I hope she's paying you well."

His dad made a dismissive wave. "We'll get to that. It's just good to have something to do, get away from the house."

So this Audrey was enjoying the fruits of his dad's labors without paying him. That wasn't exactly a point in her favor.

He only half listened as his dad kept talking about Audrey's plans for the place, all of which seemed expensive and quite possibly ill-conceived. Yes, Willow Glen got a bit of tourist traffic because of the surrounding mountains, but an out-of-the-way café seemed a risky proposition. He just hoped that a bit of carpentry help was all she'd talked his dad into. He'd hate to be put in the position of questioning his dad's financial decisions. That would go over like firecrackers during a church sermon.

The sound of a car coming up the lane drew their attention at the same time.

"That sounds like Audrey now," his dad said. "Come on. I think you're going to like her."

That remained to be seen.

When they stepped outside, the mysterious Audrey was hidden by the open trunk lid on her car. He followed his dad as he headed toward the vehicle, a nice blue Jetta not more than a couple of years old. It wasn't what he'd expected.

"We've got some more company we can put to work," his dad called to her.

"That right?" came the muffled voice from the back just before she closed the trunk.

The world seemed to slip into slow motion as each detail in front of him came into supersharp focus, none of them what he'd expected. Brady stared, at a loss for words and vaguely aware that his mouth might be hanging open. Instead of a woman more his father's age, a tall, leggy blonde stared back at him, surprise written across her lovely face.

Looked like today was going to be full of surprises.

## Chapter Two

The buckets of paint nearly slipped from Audrey's hands, but her brain reengaged in time for her to adjust her grip.

"Audrey York, this is my son, Brady."

Good heavens, if Brady Witt did indeed look like his father had at the same age, the recently departed Betty had been a very lucky woman. Tall, nicely toned, natural tan, angular features. His sandy-brown hair was a touch long and a bit messy, like he didn't have the time for a haircut or just didn't care.

"Nice to meet you," she said.

"Let me take those," Brady said as he reached for the paint cans.

"I've got them, thanks. But there are a couple of bags in the backseat with dinner in them." Thankfully, she had extra.

As she turned away and started toward the mill, she exhaled slowly, trying to get her hammering pulse under control. It wasn't the first time she'd seen a good-looking man, far from it. So why did this one in particular cause her pulse rate to go supersonic?

Long days and little sleep, that's why. Not to mention the stress of wanting to get the café up and running and lots of work standing between her and opening day. Of course, the fact that Brady Witt was drop-dead gorgeous could have something to do with the fact that her brain synapses were misfiring.

She told herself not to care how she looked in her sweaty tank top, cargo shorts and work boots, but she couldn't help smoothing her hair once she'd placed the paint cans inside. Then she shook her head at her silliness. She didn't have to look polished and professional anymore, and that's the way she'd wanted it. Willow Glen was the antidote to all the disappointments in her old life.

"You can just set those over there." She indicated the table as Brady and Nelson came in with the bags.

"Dad's been telling me all about your plans for the place," Brady said. "Seems like quite a job for one woman."

"Well, your dad has been a big help."

"So I hear."

She glanced up at Brady as she pulled the sub sandwiches and chips from the bags. Was that suspicion in his voice?

No, it couldn't be. He had no reason to suspect her of anything. She'd be glad when she stopped hearing and seeing accusations and suspicion everywhere she looked.

But even after they all sat down to eat, she couldn't

shake the feeling that he was watching her for some misstep, some clue that would shine a bright spotlight on everything she wanted to leave behind.

"So, what gave you the idea for this little venture?" Brady asked.

It didn't take a top investigator to figure out that he didn't think it would work. But that was okay. She had enough belief in the project to counter any naysayers.

"I came up here last year, did some hiking along the Willow Trail, canoed along the creek. That's when I saw this old mill, and my imagination just started leaping with ideas."

She didn't much believe in fate or destiny anymore, except what you made for yourself, but something about the sight of this old mill when she'd floated by that day had spoken to her, called her name, begged her to save it. At the time, she'd taken photos of it to preserve the piece of history. Only later did actual preservation of the building occur to her as a way of guiding her life in a new direction.

"How do you plan to get people out here?"

"Advertise in tourist publications, build a spur trail from here to the Willow Trail, construct a take-in/take-out point for canoeists on the creek here, maybe even rent canoes at some point. Trust me, I thought about this a long time and didn't jump into it lightly."

She detected surprise in the widening of Brady's greenish-gold eyes, and satisfaction bloomed inside her.

"Dad said you had a business plan. Looks like he was right. Well, good luck with everything." He broke eye contact and glanced down at the crumbs of his meal.

He might mean it, but it sounded more like a throwaway comment, something you say to someone you don't know and don't plan on getting to know. The detachment irritated her.

"Thank you." She stood and gathered all the sandwich wrappers, chip bags, napkins and paper plates from the table then deposited them in the trash can. "Well, I need to get to some paperwork."

The chairs scraped the rough wooden floor behind her.

"We'll see you bright and early in the morning," Nelson said, as he did every afternoon when he left for the day.

"Actually, Dad, I thought we might go fishing tomorrow."

"Fishing?" Nelson looked at his son as if the suggestion made no sense. "I'm in the middle of a job here."

"I'm sure Ms. York can spare you for a few days," Brady said.

"Certainly," she said with forced brightness as she turned to face them. "Spend some time with Brady."

"I can spend time with Brady here," Nelson said. "I've got to get that window area finished then start work on the tables. And with one more set of experienced hands, the work will go faster."

Brady shifted his stance like he wanted to argue, but he kept quiet. She'd give just about anything to peek inside his brain for two minutes.

"Seriously, I'm fine," she said to Nelson. "You've been a dear so far, but—"

Nelson shook his head and waved off her objection. "No. Once I start something, I finish it. I'll see you in the morning." With that, he patted her on the shoulder and headed outside, leaving her and Brady to stare after him.

She didn't meet Brady's eyes, but she felt his gaze on her.

"Thanks for dinner," he said. "Guess I'll see you in the morning."

She uttered a "good night" and watched as he disappeared out the door, too.

So he was coming back with his dad. Fantastic, an entire day, maybe days, of him watching, suspecting. Oh, yeah, this was going to be all kinds of fun.

WHEN BRADY WALKED into the house, his dad wandered out of the kitchen holding a glass of milk.

"Care to tell me what that was all about?" his dad asked.

"What?"

"How you acted with Audrey. You were nearly rude."

"I wasn't rude."

"You know I've been helping her out, and right in front of her you say you want me to go fishing instead."

"I thought it'd be nice, that's all."

Nelson raised one eyebrow. "You do remember I've been catching you in lies since you were able to talk, right?"

"It's nothing, okay? I was just surprised you'd been spending so much time with her and hadn't mentioned it." Brady tossed his bag on the couch.

"I'm thankful she's given me something to do. It's

not like I'm dating the girl. She's young enough to be my daughter."

Brady didn't respond, didn't know how.

His dad caught his eye just as he took a drink of his milk. Nelson lowered the glass. "That's what you thought, isn't it? That I'd taken up with someone already?"

Brady waved away the accusation. "No, of course not." The lie gnawed at his gut.

Anger replaced the sadness in his dad's eyes. "Don't you ever doubt how much I loved your mother. She was my one and only."

Brady shoved his hands in his pants pockets. "I know that, Dad."

"Well, if you know that, why the suspicion?"

"It's not your actions I'm worried about."

"What, you think a pretty young girl like Audrey would be after an old codger like me?" He gave Brady a raised-eyebrow look that said the very idea was the height of unlikely.

"You have a TV. You know it happens. Young women hooking up with older men for their money."

His dad actually snorted, the closest thing to a laugh Brady had heard from him in a long time, since before his mom's stroke.

"I'm old, not stupid."

"What do you really know about her, anyway?"

"I know she moved here from Nashville because she wanted to get out of the city. That she's excited about this project, is enthusiastic, a very hard worker, is addicted to the Food Network and is missing it. And she was a friend to an old man when he needed one." His dad shook his head. "I even joked with her that I was going to try to fix the two of you up. Looks like she was right."

Brady tilted his head slightly. "About what?"

"That it's a bad idea." With that, Nelson sat his empty glass on the end of the kitchen counter and headed down the hallway toward his bedroom.

Brady stood in the middle of the living room, wondering how he'd managed to handle this whole situation so badly. All he wanted to do was make sure his father was okay, that he wasn't duped. But somehow he'd turned into the bad guy. Just great. That should make the next two weeks freaking wonderful.

AFTER YET ANOTHER dreadful night of sleep, Audrey was on the steep, A-shaped roof, nailing down new pieces of silver tin roofing by six the next morning. The gentle breeze in the surrounding forest and the trickling of the creek next to the mill should have soothed her, but even they couldn't smooth her ragged edges. By the time Nelson and Brady showed up, her mood still hadn't improved.

"Lord, girl, what are you doing up there?" Nelson asked as he looked at her with his eyes shaded by his hand.

"Roofing. I've got to get this done before the electrician shows up in case it rains."

"How in the world do you know how to roof a building?"

She hesitated as she wiped the sweat from her forehead. How to answer? "I volunteered for Habitat for

Humanity after Katrina." True. No need to mention the missionary trips to developing countries when she'd helped build homes for the poorest of the poor.

Nelson pointed toward where she kneeled. "Brady, get up there and help her."

"No, really, I'm fine." The last thing she needed while perched on a roof was Mr. I'm Watching You by her side, no matter how good-looking he was.

As if to spite her determination to work alone, however, she moved her foot and accidentally sent her hammer sliding down and off the edge of the roof onto the ground below. She bit down on the expletive, not wanting to utter it in front of Nelson.

She glanced at Brady to determine his reaction. His face was hidden from her, however, as he bent to retrieve the hammer. Nelson shook his head as he headed indoors.

Audrey directed her gaze at the tree canopy above and took a few deep breaths, told herself that everything would be fine. All she needed to do was let Brady get to know her a little so the suspicion she'd seen in his eyes the day before disappeared. Maybe it was just a small-town suspicion of newcomers and nothing more. She'd have to overcome that to make her café success- ful, so she might as well start tackling it now.

Brady appeared at the top of the ladder, hammer in hand.

"Thank you," she said as he handed it to her.

Without asking, he stepped onto the roof and slid one piece of tin after another into place while she hammered.

"I can do that for a while if you like," he offered.

"Thanks, but I've got it." Actually, physical labor felt good, cathartic even.

A couple of minutes went by before he spoke again. "Did the tin do something to tick you off?" he asked, a touch of teasing in his question.

She stopped, realized thoughts of the past had caused her to start hammering harder. She leaned against the roof and wiped the sweat off her forehead again. "I just want to get done."

"Won't do you any good if you beat a hole through the roof."

Audrey stared down at her boots, frustrated that the past still had the ability to make anger pulse through her. She didn't want to be that angry, disappointed person anymore. She took several seconds to cool off and catch her breath then went back to hammering, though less violently this time.

"So, how'd you and my dad meet?" Brady asked.

She swallowed her instinctive aversion to questioning and replied in an even tone, "At the grocery store. I helped him find something he was looking for."

"And that led to him working out here every day?"

Audrey glanced at Brady. "You're the inquisitive sort, aren't you?" she asked, keeping her question light, not accusatory.

Brady sat back and propped one forearm on his upturned knee. "I'm just looking out for my dad."

"That's what I've been doing."

"Why?"

"Because he seemed like he needed it." One glance

at Brady told her that he had, indeed, simply been concerned for his recently widowed father's welfare. She remembered how lost Nelson had looked in the grocery store and understood Brady's concern. Just because the concept of a close relationship with a parent wasn't within her current realm of possibility didn't mean they didn't exist anymore. Even she had once enjoyed such a relationship.

Nelson wandered outside to dump some wood scraps into the burning barrel. Neither she nor Brady spoke until the older man stepped back inside.

"Listen, I'm not sure what you were thinking, but I'm not out to get anything from your dad. He's a nice man, and I've liked having him around. And he appears to like coming out here."

Brady stretched his legs out and leaned back on his palms. He stared toward the gentle flow of the creek. "I'm sorry. He was just acting so different from the last time I saw him."

"But that's a good thing."

Brady looked at her, questions written all over his handsome face.

"When I met your dad, he was standing in front of the cherry pie filling in the grocery store, totally overwhelmed by which one to buy. He was on the verge of tears. It made my heart break. He looked so relieved when I helped him pick a can for cobbler."

Brady lowered his head, as if he were trying to see his dad through the tin of the roof. "Mom's cobbler. It's his favorite dessert."

"I didn't know about your mom then. I thought your mom had sent him to the store to do the shopping she normally did." She told him about her conversation with Meg the cashier and her subsequent encounter with his dad in the parking lot. "I was only trying to help him in that moment. But once he came out here with those picture frames, he seemed to want to talk. The more we talked and I told him about my ideas, the more of his sadness drifted away. I mean, I still see it sometimes, but I honestly think it's good for him to stay busy. It keeps his mind on something other than how much he misses your mom."

And Audrey was the expert on staying busy to keep other thoughts at bay.

"I know. That's part of the reason I came up here. I was worried about him. He hasn't been the same person since Mom died."

"That's understandable. They were married for a long time. This isn't something you get past in a few days." She remembered the deep sorrow that had cloaked her own mother in the weeks following the unexpected death of Audrey's father.

Brady glanced up at her. "You say that like you know from experience."

She swallowed and shook away the unwanted memory. "Just common sense." She lifted the hammer and moved toward the top of the roofline. "We should try to finish this before it gets too hot. I'm already sweating like I've been jogging across Death Valley."

The old keeping-busy philosophy at work. If she

filled her mind with roofing and painting and electrical wiring, she didn't have to remember the father she'd lost. Or the mother she'd walked away from.

AUDREY YORK MIGHT NOT be after his father's money, but she was definitely hiding something. Call it gut instinct, but he'd seen something in her eyes, almost a touch of fear. Fear that he'd find out something she wanted to keep hidden? He shook his head, realized yet again that he was comparing her to a bad memory. His brain knew all women weren't like Ginny, but his gut kept missing the memo.

But he had to give credit where credit was due. She was indeed a hard worker. She was slicked with sweat, cuts and scrapes covered her hands and knees, her hair was coming loose from her ponytail, and she didn't pay any of it a moment of attention. Her single-minded focus stayed on getting this roof completed in record time.

He paused for a moment to watch her hammer. Even disheveled, she was a beauty. And she acted like she was either unaware of that fact or didn't care. Before his work pants became uncomfortable, he pulled another piece of tin into place.

"Dad said you moved from Nashville. Did you run a restaurant there?"

Audrey made one last strike of the hammer before shifting to the right and the next piece of tin. "No." She paused to lift her sweaty face to what little breeze was stirring the air. She seemed to hesitate before continuing. "I was a fund-raiser."

Fund-raiser to restaurant owner—odd transition. So was Nashville to Willow Glen.

"What about you?" she asked. "I hear you have a construction company or something."

Brady noticed how she deflected the focus back to him, how she seemed unaware of how big Witt Construction was. Maybe he'd just acknowledge the small Kingsport location and see how she reacted. "Half of one. My partner, Craig, owns the other half." He caught the quick, questioning glance she tossed his way. "That's business partner, not *partner* partner."

She laughed. "You guys are so overly sensitive about that topic."

"Just clarifying." Wow, she should definitely smile more often. It rocketed her from beautiful to stunning.

"What?"

The questioning look on her face told him he'd been staring again. She had that effect on him. "Nothing. I was thinking you seem to be in a safer mood now that you're not trying to murder the tin with that hammer."

She held up the tool in question and stared at it. "Guess I worked out most of the frustration I was feeling."

He held up a hand, palm out. "Remind me to never frustrate you."

Damn, he was flirting. He wasn't here to get a date. He'd left a pile of his own work behind to make sure his dad was okay. But he'd done that and yet here he still was, working for no pay. Seemed his dad was no longer the only person on his mind.

Audrey shook the hammer at him in mock threat, then went back to her task.

Just because he wasn't looking to hook up didn't mean he couldn't enjoy the view while he worked.

They were putting the last piece of tin on one side of the roof in place when a racket and then a string of curses came from inside the mill. They nearly tripped over each other getting to and down the ladder. When they rushed inside, Nelson was holding his hand and still uttering a few choice words.

"What's wrong?" Audrey rushed toward Nelson.

"Ah, I smashed my finger with the hammer."

"Let me see."

Brady watched as Audrey took his dad's hand in hers, turned it over carefully and examined it. Something shifted inside him at the gentleness and concern. He didn't think anyone could fake with that much authenticity.

"We need to take you to the emergency room, make sure you haven't broken anything," Audrey said.

His dad moved his hand out of hers. "No need for that. It's nothing."

"It's turning a nice shade of eggplant," she argued, her hands on her hips.

"Honey, if I'd gone to the hospital every time I smashed my fingers, I'd have funded an entire new wing by now."

Brady smiled, glad to see more and more of the dad he'd always known coming back to the light of day.

"At least let me get you an ice pack."

"Okay, if it'll make *you* feel better," Nelson said with a teasing smile.

"It's supposed to make *you* feel better, you stubborn old man." She shook her head, acting exasperated with him.

Brady tried to hide a laugh but didn't fully succeed.

"What are you laughing at?" his dad asked. "You get over there and finish up what I started. And try not to hit your finger. She'll be hauling us both off to the E.R."

Audrey swatted Nelson on the upper arm as she headed for the cooler in the corner. After fixing Nelson an ice pack and sitting him in a lawn chair in the corner, Audrey pulled a couple of bottles of water out of the ice. She tossed one to Brady as he moved toward the window frame his father had been constructing.

Brady turned in time to see Audrey down about half her water before coming up for air. Condensation from the bottom of the bottle dropped onto her chest and rolled downward toward the scoop of her tank top. Brady's skin heated, and he licked his lips before he could think not to.

"Ow." Brady winced at the sudden pain in his leg and turned around to find his dad giving him the look he always used when he'd found Brady misbehaving. So the old man hadn't missed his gawking.

"What?" Audrey asked as she rolled her cold bottle of water to her forehead.

"Nothing," Nelson said. "Just giving the boy a little nudge."

Yeah, if you called a kick to the calf with a steel-toed work boot a nudge.

Staring at warm, enticing female flesh wasn't a problem after Audrey returned to the roof. Thing was, he was hotter now than he'd been sitting on tin with the sun beating down on him.

His dad walked across the room, moving to the open doorway in Brady's peripheral vision.

"She's a good girl. Don't trifle if you don't really like her."

Nelson stepped outside without giving Brady the chance to respond that he had no intention of *trifling*. Dang, all he'd done was look. He was a red-blooded male, young, healthy, single. When a beautiful woman was nearby, he tended to notice. But anything beyond that with someone his dad considered a friend had *bad idea* written all over it. Because Brady wasn't a long-term kind of guy—not anymore.

An engine started outside, and it only took a moment for Brady to realize it was his truck. By the time he reached the door, his dad was heading down the lane toward the road.

First his dad told him to steer clear of Audrey then he left the two of them alone. What was the old guy up to?

# Chapter Three

Audrey sat back on her heels and watched as Brady deposited some useless bits of wood in the burning barrel.

"Where'd your dad go?"

He shrugged. "Heck if I know. He just took off."

"That's odd. Was he feeling bad?"

"No more than a throbbing finger. Need some help?"

She nearly declined, but honestly she was pooped and the initial tension between her and Brady had eased. At least the tension regarding his father. The other tension on her part wouldn't fade unless Brady fell out of the ugly tree and hit every branch on the way down. "Sure."

Brady climbed the ladder and made his way over to her side of the roof. "This may qualify as the fastest roofing job ever."

"It's only going to get hotter, and I don't fancy roasting into a lobster up here or going broke buying sunscreen. The curse of the blond." She gestured toward her hair.

After getting another piece of roofing in place and

attached, Audrey lay back. "I am one hundred and ten percent wiped. I feel like I could lie in the grass and sleep for about two days."

"We're almost done. Come on."

With a moan, she raised herself and got back to work. "This can't be your idea of a good time on vacation."

"It's not really vacation. Seems like Dad's doing okay though, so maybe I should just go back home."

Audrey retrieved a nail and set it in place while trying to ignore the thought that she'd miss seeing his face. "Do you have something pressing at work?"

"There's always something pressing at work."

"Something your *business* partner can't handle?"

He glanced over at her, gave her a half smile at the focus she put on the word *business*. "No."

"Then maybe you should just hang out with your dad. I'm sure he enjoys being with you. And he might not say anything or act like it, but I suspect he needs the company when he goes home at night."

"He seemed surprisingly okay last night, except for the scolding I got for being rude to you."

Her eyes widened as she looked at him. "Scolding? At your age? How embarrassing." She pressed her lips together to stifle a giggle at the image.

Brady snorted. "Guess I deserved it."

"Don't worry about it. I understand your wanting to look out for your dad."

After all, there were people out there more than willing to bilk others out of their hard-earned money. She knew that firsthand.

THEY FINISHED attaching the roofing but left applying the sealant for another day and climbed down the ladder. Brady followed Audrey to the side of the creek, where she untied and removed her boots and socks then slipped her feet into the flowing water.

"Ah!" She flopped back into the grass, letting the water bob her feet. "I may never move again."

"You'll move. The ants, mosquitoes and chiggers will eventually find you and have you for lunch."

"Oh, fine, ruin the moment," she said in a light, teasing tone.

This was definitely better than suspicion and animosity. So she was hiding something. Who didn't have secrets? It didn't mean it was anything aimed at hurting him or his dad. Roasting hot himself, Brady gave in to temptation and shucked his boots and socks, too. After rolling up his pant legs to the knees, he stuck his feet in the water and lay back in the grass only a couple of feet from Audrey.

"I haven't done this in years," he said.

She turned her head to look at him. "What, stuck your feet in the creek?"

"Yeah. That and just lie in the grass, looking up at the trees."

Audrey let out a slow sigh as she returned her gaze to the sky above. "Guess we forget the simple ways to enjoy life when we grow up."

"That why you bought this place? To enjoy life?"

"It just felt right. I woke up one morning and realized I needed a change."

"Was your job boring?"

She didn't answer immediately. He glanced toward her, but she was still staring toward the treetops high above them.

"I was between jobs. Seemed like the right time to ask myself what I really wanted. Only, I had no idea what that might be. I went for a walk one afternoon, and I somehow ended up at a bookstore. I don't even know why I went in, but I found myself standing in front of the magazine section. I started flipping through different magazines, and this story about a woman who refurbished an old lighthouse and made a B & B out of it caused something to click inside me. Needless to say, not a lot of lighthouses in Tennessee. But that's when I remembered this mill. I had no interest in a B & B, but I love to cook and thought, why not a café?"

She turned her head and met his eyes. "And that's way more info than you asked for."

"It's okay. Saves me the trouble of asking more questions."

She huffed out a laugh. "You have your dad's sense of humor."

"Really? I've been accused of having no sense of humor."

"Everyone has one, some just deeper than others."

He returned his gaze to the sky peeking through the trees. Something about her confession about her life unsettled him. Was it that she had indeed shared too much of herself with him? He'd turned into a surface-relationship kind of guy, much to his family's disappointment. Nothing too serious. Not that he and Audrey had or would have a relationship beyond temporary coworkers.

"So why didn't you hire roofers?" he asked.

"I like my arm and my leg, thanks. The cost of the electrician and the plumber is going to kill me as it is. Plus, I like to do things for myself as much as I can."

"Hey, I bet you have contacts from being in fundraising. Maybe you could find an investor for your business."

"No." She didn't yell or snap, but he heard the strength and finality behind the single word even before Audrey suddenly rose to her feet.

"Did I say something wrong?"

"No, you're fine. Enjoy the creek. I just have a lot of work to do."

The water sloshed as he lifted his feet out and stood, too. "Audrey, what's wrong?" Had his bad memories caused him to say something he shouldn't without realizing it?

"Time is money. I don't need to be lying around surveying the past, not when I have a blue bazillion tasks with my name on them."

He watched her retrieve her boots and socks and stalk off toward the mill. He searched back over their conversation but couldn't figure out what had altered the mood so drastically.

Women. Their moods shifted more than a house built on clay.

BRADY PROBABLY THOUGHT she'd lost her mind, and perhaps she was a bit crazy when it came to asking for money for herself. She simply didn't do it. She hadn't even applied for a bank loan to finance the purchase and refurbishing of the mill. Instead, she had liquidated accounts and sold the possessions she could live without. She was doing this alone, even if she had to get another job to make her dream come true. Even if she had to make her last penny scream for mercy.

No one would ever be able to accuse her of being like her mother.

She sank onto the stairs leading to the loft and pressed against the pressure building behind her forehead. What she'd told Brady about why she'd left her life was only partially true. But she wasn't about to tell him that she'd simply gotten tired of people always watching her, wondering if she would yet prove to be her mother's daughter in action as well as genetics. Part of the allure of Willow Glen was that no one evidently knew who she was beyond her identity as the newest resident. And she hoped it stayed that way.

When she heard Brady step back into the mill, she rose and climbed the rest of the way up to the loft. Once there, though, she felt trapped with nothing productive to do. She'd already crunched the numbers half a dozen times, and she couldn't really start refurbishing the living space until the plumber and electrician completed their respective tasks.

It was too blasted hot to apply sealant to the roof, and she was too antsy to spend time in the same room as

Brady. She'd really like to grab her camera gear and head off into the woods to photograph some wildflowers, a hobby that never failed to bring her joy. After all, she had all those beautiful, handmade frames to fill. But with so much to do, she knew she wouldn't fully enjoy the outing. Time was money, and she wasn't exactly awash in either.

She walked over to the small loft door. It would eventually become a window overlooking a bend in the creek beyond the mill and the long line of weeping willows lining the bank. She envisioned a gazebo in that bend complete with a table and chairs for special, private meals for guests.

Inspired, she grabbed her notebook of ideas and started sketching the gazebo and the surroundings. She pictured it white in contrast to the greens of the trees shading it, covered in twinkling white lights, a quaint table with two chairs in its center. A romantic spot for couples on a special date. She smiled as she imagined marriage proposals being offered there by nervous grooms-to-be.

She might not be lucky in love, but she had a romantic streak several miles wide. And this gazebo idea had it humming. Even though she should be focusing all her energy on the mill and not adding even more expenses, she couldn't dampen the enthusiasm. The desire to go buy twinkling lights, tulle for the gazebo's ceiling and magazines with gazebo designs rushed through her, but she forced her attention back to her list of priorities. With the structural work progressing well, she needed to go buy the lumber necessary for the construction of the kitchen in the back corner next to the stairs. She estimated it was time to look at appliances, as well.

After all, she was at a standstill on the mill until the electrician came tomorrow morning. Maybe she could get some landscaping flowers for the area around the front of the mill, and a couple of hanging pots.

Okay, she had to stop her runaway brain before she imagined herself right into debt.

She grabbed her keys and purse and headed for the stairs. When she reached the bottom, she noticed Brady leaning against the railing around the mill's machinery, wiping the sweat from his face with a paper towel. She swallowed when she saw how his damp T-shirt molded to his honest-work muscles. For a shocking moment, she pictured her and Brady in that fairy-tale gazebo before she looked away and mentally smacked herself upside the head.

"Where you off to?" he asked.

"Need some supplies. I think I'll drive down to Elizabethton."

"Mind if I ride along? The last piece of framing I have isn't quite long enough. We could use it for a smaller window, but not this one. And since the old man left me without wheels…"

So much for the peace of a solo trip. She forced herself not to scream at his self-invitation. As if to spite her efforts to avoid him, now she was going to be trapped in a small, confined space with him for the twenty miles to Elizabethton and back.

"Sure. We'll get enough to do the window upstairs, too, while we're at it. And make sure we get the best lumber for the kitchen."

"Do you have the measurements for the upstairs window?"

"Yeah." She patted her purse where she kept her running to-buy list. "Right here with your dad's specs for the kitchen."

"She's on the ball," he said as he pushed away from the railing.

It was hardly a romantic compliment, but she couldn't help how her skin warmed as she met his gaze. Seriously, she should have dunked her head in the creek instead of her feet.

"You DO KNOW that Christmas is seven months away, right?"

Audrey glanced up from her spot in the garden section at Lowe's as Brady wheeled the cart with the lumber needed for the window up next to her. He looked so at home here, in the middle of a warehouse full of home-improvement ecstasy.

"They're for the gazebo, not a Christmas tree," she said as she placed several boxes of stringed white lights in the cart. At his confused expression, she flipped open one of the magazines she held and showed him a beautiful gazebo decorated for weddings. "Guys find these things cheesy, but women will love a romantic gazebo by the creek, a private dining area for couples." She looked at the picture again and smiled at the magic the simple picture conveyed. "We might even have weddings there." She was trying to cram as much happiness and positive energy into her life as possible, and what could be happier than a wedding?

She hadn't planned to buy anything for the gazebo today. But when she'd finished ordering what she needed and found Brady busy at the contractors' counter, she'd gravitated to the garden center, where her imagination got the best of her.

"Does your brain crank out ideas even when you're sleeping?" Brady asked, sounding amazed and amused at the same time.

"As a matter of fact, it does." She laughed and tossed the magazines into the cart. "I wake up in the middle of the night and have to jot them down before I forget them."

They started down the aisle as Brady shook his head once. "Sounds like it makes for terrible sleeping."

"I'm not a very restful sleeper anyway."

At least not since her life had been turned upside down and inside out more than a year ago. That memory dampened her enthusiasm, so she headed for the outdoor part of the garden center, hoping that immersing herself in colorful, fragrant flowers would lift her mood again.

As they moved up and down the aisles, she selected several flats of impatiens in a variety of bright colors, a couple of gorgeous hanging baskets filled with purple petunias and a rose trellis for the bush she'd noticed at the back of the mill.

"You know, if you're going to put that gazebo in the creek bend, you might want to make a stone path to it from the drive, for when the ground is wet." Brady pointed out shelves filled with different-colored stepping-stones.

Another unexpected expense, the type she suspected Brady wouldn't think twice about, but a good idea nonetheless. "So, what do you think, the gray or the red?"

Brady ran his fingers over the surface of the rock slabs in question, and an unexpected warmth flowed along Audrey's arms at the thought of those long fingers doing the same thing to her skin.

Maybe she had stayed in the sun too long that morning and baked her brain. She felt like she was experiencing Brady overload. She'd caught herself snatching glimpses of him ever since they'd arrived at the store, glimpses she didn't dare in the car because he would have noticed. But each time she looked at him, the more attractive he became. The archetypal sexy carpenter. She wondered if he looked as good as she imagined in nothing but a pair of jeans and a tool belt.

What was wrong with her? Hadn't Darren's desertion taught her anything?

But Brady wasn't Darren.

Still, she couldn't risk getting too involved, not when it could put everything she had and was trying to build at risk.

"The gray."

"Huh?" Audrey zipped back from Fantasy World and stared at Brady, wondering what he was talking about.

"The stepping-stones." He pointed. When she didn't react, he pecked against the stone with his fingertip. "Hello?"

"Oh, yeah. I think you're right. They'll go better with the surroundings. That's way down the list of priorities though."

"Where were you a moment ago?"

"Sorry, brief side trip to la-la land." Trying to dispel the jittery feeling threatening to overtake her, she took a few steps away from Brady and grabbed two pairs of gardening gloves hanging from a shelf. "You finished with your business?"

"Yeah."

"Well, hello there," a silver-haired lady said as she guided her cart up next to theirs.

"Hi, Miss Brenda," Brady said as he gave the woman a quick hug. "How are you?"

"If I was any better, I don't know how I'd be able to stand it," she said with a big smile. She looked at Audrey. "Are you a friend of Brady's?"

"This is Audrey York," Brady said. "Dad and I are doing some work for her. Audrey, this is Brenda Phillips. She was my sixth-grade teacher."

"Oh, you must be the little gal who bought the old mill," Brenda said. "I've got to tell you, the ladies at church are already twittering about that."

Audrey's breath caught. But if this woman knew who she really was, why would she be smiling and acting friendly?

"It'll be so nice to have someplace quaint to have

lunch with the girls," Miss Brenda said, giving Audrey's hand a gentle squeeze. "You need to come to service next Sunday, meet all the ladies. Good way to start getting to know your neighbors and potential customers."

Audrey managed a smile. "Thank you for the invitation." Though the idea of stepping back into a church left her cold. Of course, that was due to what had happened with her mother and not the church itself.

"Well, I best be getting home." Miss Brenda pointed at the items in her cart. "Sam is anxious to get these plants in the ground." With another genuine smile and a wave, Brenda headed for the checkout.

"She's a bit of a whirlwind, isn't she?" Brady said.

"You could say that."

Brady laughed a little at what must be her stunned expression then pushed their shopping cart toward the front of the store, too.

Audrey eyed the items in the cart. Boy, had she gone overboard.

"Don't worry. We'll make it all fit," Brady said, guessing at her thoughts.

They did, barely. The trellis stuck out of the tied-down trunk, and flowers appeared to have taken root in her backseat.

Brady looked across the top of the car at her. "You hungry?"

"Yeah, but let's do lunch on the cheap. I'm pretty sure I just heard my credit card whimper."

"Pal's, it is." He bumped his knuckles against the car's roof.

"Pal's?"

He eyed her with disbelief. "You haven't been there yet?"

"No, should I have?"

"You haven't lived until you've had a Pal's chipped ham and cheese sandwich and seasoned fries."

She uttered a little laugh. "Well, I certainly want to live."

"Get in the car and drive, then, woman."

Brady directed her to a spot on Elk Avenue. She laughed when she caught sight of the blue concrete-block building with a giant hot dog, fries and drink cup on the roof.

"Don't let the outside fool you," Brady said. "Eat Pal's once and you're a slave to it for life."

Audrey gave the structure a doubtful look. "If you say so."

They ordered on one side of the building then drove around to the other to pay and get their food. Her stomach growled when she handed the bag to Brady.

"See, your stomach knows good food is in the vicinity. Drive down the street. We can eat at the park."

The park ended up being Sycamore Shoals State Park, complete with a reconstructed eighteenth-century fort. With the beautiful, late-May day as a backdrop, the slice of the area's history captured Audrey's fascination.

"I wish I'd brought my camera," she said.

"You can come back when they're doing garrison weekends. Seems more like you're stepping into history with everyone dressed in costume."

Brady led her past the fort and toward a trail.

"Where are we going?"

"You'll see."

Wasn't he Mr. Mysterious all of a sudden? It seemed a bit out of character based on what little she knew about him.

It wasn't long before she heard rushing water then saw an expanse of gentle river rapids. The river was probably three times the width of Willow Creek, but in spots she wasn't sure it was as deep.

"This is gorgeous," she said as she stepped to the edge of the bank.

"Welcome to the Sycamore Shoals of the Watauga River."

"No wonder they built a fort here." She edged right up next to the clear water and looked both upstream and down. Again, she wished for her camera.

"Since you liked the old mill, I figured you'd like this, too." Brady led the way to a rocky outcropping. They sat and pulled their lunch from the bag. "This was the first permanent settlement outside the thirteen original colonies."

"Sounds like you know a lot about it."

"Craig's dad is one of the historic reenactors when they have living-history weekends. I went to a million of them when I was growing up."

Audrey unfolded a napkin on the rock and placed her food on top of it. "So, you and Craig have been friends a long time?"

"Since fourth grade when he moved to Willow Glen from Bristol."

Audrey formulated another question as she stuck a couple of fries in her mouth. The question disappeared as flavor woke up her taste buds.

"Mmm, these are good fries." She licked the seasoning from her fingers.

"Told you." Brady smiled in an all-knowing way.

When Audrey took a bite of her ham and cheese sandwich, she closed her eyes and made a sound of appreciation.

Brady laughed. "Another Pal's devotee is born."

"I'm fairly sure my waistline is going to curse you forever, but right now I don't care."

"You've got nothing to worry about," he said before turning his attention to the river and a large piece of driftwood floating by.

What had that comment meant exactly? Was it a compliment about her physical appearance or more of a comment that women worried too much?

For a few minutes, they ate with only the sound of the rapids filling the air between them. Audrey relished the unexpected peace that settled on her.

"I think I could sit here all day," she said.

"It's tempting sometimes. You know, Willow Creek empties into this river."

An older couple walked by hand in hand on the trail behind Audrey and Brady. After they passed, Audrey watched them, smiled at how in love they looked after what might have been years of marriage, children and grandchildren.

"They're cute," she said.

"Mom and Dad were like that. Used to embarrass me and Sophie when we were kids."

A wistfulness in Brady's voice caused Audrey to turn toward him. "They loved each other a lot, didn't they?"

"Yeah. Craig used to come over all the time. He couldn't believe how well my parents got along."

"His didn't?"

Brady shook his head. "They had a nasty divorce right before he and his dad moved here. I think he's only seen his mom a couple of times since then."

"That's sad." Though death had separated her own parents, she felt an immediate kinship with Craig, the kind born of growing up with only one parent. And of being estranged from their mothers.

"Yeah, but he's probably better off. I was lucky, but sometimes it's better for people to split up and move on."

Audrey ate the last two fries from the bottom of the bag and wondered, not for the first time, how her life might have been different if her dad hadn't died. Would her mother have still turned out to be the person she had? Or had the loss of her husband changed her in some irrevocable way?

"What about your parents? They still together?"

Why hadn't she steered clear of this topic? Now she couldn't veer away without the word *obvious* writing itself across her forehead in huge, capital letters.

"My dad died of a heart attack when I was little, and…Mom and I aren't close. We don't talk often." Like ever, not in the past year, anyway. Not since her mother had been charged with fraud.

"Sorry."

She waved away his concern. "It's okay. Like you said, you were lucky. Seems the happy nuclear family is an endangered species."

He made what sounded like a grunt of agreement.

A man and two little boys picked their way to the edge of the river several yards downstream. The boys, who looked to be about four years old and twins, started throwing sticks and rocks into the water.

Adorable little kids, something else life might not have in store for her. But after the conversation of the past few minutes, did she even want to subject more children to the cruelty of life and the fickleness of relationships?

Enough of this downer stuff. She was making a good life for herself, one filled with hope and beauty and not tainted by the past. Maybe even some new friendships, she thought as she glanced at Brady. That's all she could hope for now. It had to be enough.

"We should get back. I want to get some of those flowers in the ground," she said.

They walked back through the interior of the fort and the visitor center. On the way out the front door toward the parking lot, a headline in the *USA TODAY* box caught her attention.

More Arrests Possible in Evangelist Fraud Case.

Her heart stumbled painfully, as if it'd tripped on a big root and crashed to the packed earth. Pulse pounding in her ears, she leaned forward and read the opening of the article.

*Investigators have found new evidence in the fraud*

*case of former evangelist Thomasina York, which may lead to more arrests.*

Audrey felt the hated tightness in her chest right before her air passages constricted and her lungs started wheezing. Dizziness swamped her. She grabbed at the newspaper box, but her fingers slipped off the edge. She opened her mouth in an effort to suck in needed air as she felt her arms and legs go weak with tingling.

Just when she thought the nightmare was behind her, it came barreling into her new life.

# Chapter Four

Brady turned around at Audrey's sound of distress to see her gasping and stumbling backward. He sprang to catch her before she fell and hurt herself. With his arm wrapped around her shoulders, he guided her back a few steps to a bench then knelt in front of her.

"Audrey, what's wrong?" As soon as he asked, he heard the wheezing and saw her struggling to get it under control.

"Asthma," she said between wheezes. "I'll be okay…in a minute."

She didn't look okay. Totally freaked was more like it.

"Do you have an inhaler?"

"At home."

Where it would do her no good. But he wasn't going to scold her now when she couldn't breathe. He stood and pulled her to her feet, then started to lift her in his arms.

She took a step away. "What are you doing?" she gasped.

"Taking you to the hospital." And fast.

She waved away his concern. "I'm fine."

"You don't sound fine. You're having an asthma attack, and you have no inhaler."

"Really—"

"You're going. That's final."

She gave up arguing, either feeling it was futile or re-alizing she needed the help. But she didn't let him carry her, instead making her way slowly to the car and falling into the passenger seat.

Brady slid the driver's seat back to accommodate his longer legs and started the ignition in the same motion. He ran one stoplight and nearly creamed a squirrel racing across the street, but he didn't care.

Audrey's breathing sounded less labored by the time he braked outside the E.R. doors, but he wasn't taking any chances. He honked several times, then raced to her side of the car to help her out.

A nurse hurried out the door. "What's the emergency?"

Brady looked across the top of the Jetta. "She's having an asthma attack."

Audrey tried to protest again, but her words were drowned out by the activity of hospital staff guiding her into a wheelchair, hurrying her inside and pumping him for details.

"Is she allergic to anything?" another nurse asked.

"I don't know," Brady said, feeling useless.

Once inside the E.R., he was steered in one direction as Audrey was wheeled off in another. He answered the nurse's questions as best he could, but that wasn't very well. All he could offer was what had happened in the minutes leading up to the attack.

"I'm sorry. We only met a few days ago. She just moved to the area."

"Maybe she's allergic to something here she's not been exposed to before." The nurse, a cherub-cheeked woman of about fifty, patted his hand. "Don't worry. We'll take good care of her. Why don't you have a seat over in the waiting area."

How in the world was he supposed to sit still when Audrey couldn't breathe? And when bad memories still lingered in this very hospital? It seemed only yesterday that he'd been here hoping his mother would recover from her stroke, here that he'd heard the doctor say that she had succumbed after lingering for a week. He wouldn't have guessed he'd be back here so soon.

THE WHEEZING WAS GONE now, replaced by embarrassment. She hadn't had an attack in months. It hadn't even occurred to her to bring her albuterol inhaler. She'd thought she was past ever needing it again.

The young doctor listened to Audrey's lungs. "You seem to be doing much better."

Audrey nodded.

"Any idea what set off the attack?"

"Anxiety. I was diagnosed with anxiety-induced asthma last year." Not to mention the occasional panic attack, but she wasn't going to share that tidbit. She didn't want to admit, even to herself, that she was still susceptible to them. Today would be the last one. It *would*.

The doctor glanced toward the door of the examining room. "Anything we can help you with?"

It took Audrey a moment to pick up on the implication. "Oh, it's not him. It's a family matter."

"He's not family?"

"No, just a…friend. He's helping me do some work on my place."

Her response must have rung true with the doctor, because the suspicion faded from her expression.

"You need to always carry your albuterol with you," she said as she gave Audrey a sample inhaler. "Even if you never need it, it's there if you do."

Audrey nodded, hating the idea of carrying around yet another reminder of how her life had changed since her mother's indictment. As she slid off the examining table, her new, beautiful life felt like a shaky lie.

As she approached the waiting area, though, she forced all those memories of the past away and put on her best "I'm totally fine" face.

Brady pushed away from the wall he was leaning against when he saw her. "You okay?"

"Good as new." She held up the inhaler and wiggled it. "And prepared for the next time high pollen counts stage a sneak attack."

"I'm sorry."

She looked at him more closely, scrunching her forehead. "What for?"

"You must have been allergic to something at the park."

Again, she waved away his concern. "Who could know? I should have had my inhaler with me." She headed for the E.R. doors, noticing that Brady had moved her car into one of the nearby parking spaces. "I don't know about you, but I'm ready for an ice-cream cone before I head back to work."

"Maybe you should take the rest of the day off," he said as he strode out beside her.

"Nah. Really, I'm fine." She took a long, deep breath. "See, no wheezing."

He didn't look comfortable about it, but he didn't protest further. Instead, he slid into the passenger side of the car without trying to baby her more by insisting on driving.

After taking a detour through the Dairy Queen drive-through, they headed back to Willow Glen. Thankfully, she was able to keep the conversation focused on the work at the mill and her plans for the future. She wanted to keep looking forward and ignore what was behind her.

If the investigators mentioned in that article would let her.

As they approached Willow Glen, Audrey looked to her left and saw a large sign set back off the road that said Witt Construction. Beyond it was a drive leading back to several buildings and a lot filled with construction machinery.

She glanced over at Brady, her eyes widening in surprise. "Is that your company?" That was a bit more than a little construction business.

"Yep. Dad started the company forty years ago."

"Looks like it must be successful." Her tone made that sound like an understatement.

"It pays the bills," he said simply. "No one's really rich in this area."

"Just good, honest, hardworking folks," she said. "That's why I like it."

After dropping Brady off at his father's house, Audrey backtracked to Willow Glen to buy a copy of the newspaper that had sent her into that horrible gasping fit. She refused to look at it, though, until she reached the mill, unloaded the supplies, poured herself a glass of lemonade and seated herself on the front porch.

With a deep breath, she opened the paper and read the article by the light of the fading day. This time, she managed not to wheeze her way through the lead, though her chest felt tight by the time she was done. Not due to asthma this time, but from pure worry. Further interviews with unnamed sources had put investigators back on the trail.

Who could they be after? Carol, her mom's personal accountant? Adam, her longtime assistant? Someone else in the ministry? Audrey had a hard time picturing any of them dipping their hands in the cash-filled cookie jar, but then her mom had shocked her, hadn't she? And if the investigators had invaded all of their lives like they had hers, how could any rock be left unturned? How could the investigators have missed anything?

Her stomach churned at the idea that those investigators might show up here asking those same horrible questions all over again. What if they showed up when Nelson was here? Or Brady? She couldn't stand the thought of having his initial suspicion of her vindicated, even if it had nothing to do with his dad.

Willow Glen was a small town, and it wouldn't take any time for word to spread. Her dream would be destroyed before she even finished the renovations. She glanced at her mother's name, and not for the first time wondered why she hadn't changed her own last name. It would put one more barrier between her and the life she wanted to leave behind. But every time she considered it, the change seemed too drastic. Not to mention it'd be a slap against the father she'd loved dearly but lost so young.

She folded the paper and stared out toward the forest surrounding the mill, watched as butterflies flitted amongst the last rays of sun slanting through the trees. She'd never sat anywhere so peaceful, and she wished she could lock the rest of the world out of her little utopia. Well, except for Nelson and Brady.

She closed her eyes and listened to the trickle of the creek to her left. It reminded her of that afternoon's picnic on the banks of the Watauga River. She'd had a really nice time with Brady.

If only things were different, she'd be more than interested in getting to know Brady Witt better. If only things were different.

AFTER YET ANOTHER bad night of sleep, Audrey dragged herself out of bed as daylight was creeping into the clearing around the mill. It was one of those mornings when she wished she was a coffee drinker, when she couldn't sleep but didn't feel fully awake, either. After eating a banana and drinking a bottle of water, she pulled on a pair of her new gardening gloves and got to work putting the flowers she'd bought the day before in the ground. She alternated colors along the edges of the porch and down the side of the mill that would be most visible to guests. They looked wilted after a day spent in the backseat of her car, but some water, fresh soil and mountain air should revive them.

She finished planting the last pot right as Nelson and Brady pulled up the lane. Even though she'd known it was likely them, she'd tensed when the sound of tires on gravel had first reached her. Visions of police cruisers or an FBI agent in an unmarked government sedan had tormented her during sleep, and it didn't appear that those same images were going to leave her alone during her waking hours.

Maybe she should call her attorney just to see if he'd heard anything, but that seemed like inviting in the bogeyman, so she scrapped the idea and decided to live with the uncertainty.

"Girl, do you ever sleep?" Nelson asked as he walked toward the mill.

"Sleep? Who needs sleep?"

Nelson snorted and headed inside to get to work on the window next to the waterwheel. Audrey glanced over at Brady and found him watching her, concern etching his features.

"You feeling okay today?" he asked.

She couldn't have him tiptoeing around her, thinking her frail, so she went the teasing route. "Yes, are *you?*"

Her response made him lift his eyebrows. "Yeah, why?"

"Because you have this look on your face like you're trying to figure out advanced calculus."

Brady loosened his stance. "That can't be a pleasant look considering I never took calculus."

"I did. Trust me, it sucked." Before she gave in to the temptation to engage him in further conversation, she walked toward the back of the mill with the intent of pulling weeds.

While Audrey felt Brady watching her every now and then as the morning went on, he was less chatty today. For the most part, they stuck to their own tasks—him helping his dad with the large window, and her working with first the electrician and then the plumber.

The only break she took was when she drove into town to buy them the pizza she'd ordered for lunch. When she walked into the Glen Grocery, Meg of the magenta hair was at the register again looking bored out of her mind. Audrey gave her a wave as she headed toward the deli in the back corner of the store where you could get everything from sliced meats to fried chicken to humongous pizzas.

The pretty, twentysomething woman working in the deli slid the pizza onto the counter for Audrey before she asked for it. She guessed word had gotten around about her and the mill project. She suspected her and Brady's encounter with Miss Brenda at Lowe's had something to do with that.

"One extra-large supreme," the woman said

Audrey glanced at her name tag. Like the rest of the

name tags at the Glen Grocery, it was topped by a yellow smiley face. Below that was the name Tewanda Hardy. "Thanks, Tewanda."

"You need somebody to come out and help you serve it? I hear Brady Witt is working for you, and I bet he looks even hotter all sweaty and dirty," Tewanda said as she fanned herself dramatically.

The statement shocked Audrey into speechlessness for a moment, until she realized that the expression on Tewanda's face was pure teasing instead of that of a woman on a mission to capture Brady. Audrey pushed down the crazy possessiveness Tewanda's words had caused to rise up in her. "No, I'm pretty sure the guys will just inhale this before I even set the box down."

Tewanda laughed. "Isn't that the truth? Men, no table manners. It's like serving wild dogs."

Audrey laughed, too, and realized she liked Tewanda despite her obvious appreciation for Brady's male form.

Tewanda placed a ticket on the pizza box and said goodbye before Audrey headed toward the checkout.

Meg perked up as Audrey approached. "Say, when are you going to open the café?"

"I'm not sure, hopefully by midsummer. Depends on how the renovations go."

"So, have you hired any waitresses yet?"

"No. You interested?" Audrey tried picturing that magenta hair inside her café, and oddly it seemed to fit.

"Yes," the girl breathed as she rang up the pizza and accepted Audrey's money. "If I stay here much longer, I may go lock myself in the freezer in the back."

Audrey glanced around at the scattering of customers in the aisles. "Boring?"

"To the nth degree."

Audrey smiled. "I tell you what. Write down your full name and phone number, and I'll be sure to call you when I'm ready to hire."

"You, Miss York, are a godsend." Meg quickly wrote her information on the back of a discarded cash register receipt and handed it over.

Audrey glanced at the paper. "I think godsend is stretching it. And call me Audrey."

When she got back to the mill, Audrey couldn't help but giggle when the guys dived at the pizza like those wild dogs Tewanda had mentioned. With a shake of her head, she grabbed a piece of the pizza before it was all gone. She ate it with one hand while she measured out the pathway to the still-nonexistent gazebo and calculated how many stepping-stones she'd eventually need.

When Nelson and Brady finished the window project, they moved on to enclosing what would be the café's kitchen in the back corner of the mill. She got on her cell and started making calls with the aim of getting the waterwheel operational again.

With that checked off her list, she carried the day's debris to the burning barrel then lit it. The more she kept busy, the less she could think about how all this work might be for nothing.

After depositing a handful of lumber scraps in the fire, she turned to get another load and almost ran into Brady. He wrapped his hand around her upper arm, as if to steady her. The moment his hand touched her bare skin, she'd swear she felt and heard a sizzle. In danger of staring into his eyes way too long, she lowered her gaze.

"Sorry, didn't hear you." She was surprised she could hear now past the hammering of her pulse.

He lowered his arm to his side, and Audrey fought the crazy feeling of being abandoned.

"Maybe that's because you've been going ninety miles an hour all day."

She looked past him, wishing her heart would stop thumping so hard against her ribs. "Lots to do."

"None of which will get done if you land back in the hospital with heatstroke. You need to slow down."

"I'm fine." She started to walk around him, but he caught her wrist, not painfully, but firm nonetheless.

"What's wrong?"

She swallowed and tried to ignore the feel of those strong fingers against her skin, how long it'd been since anyone had touched her. "Nothing. I'm just busy. I want to open this place as soon as possible."

He shook his head. "You've been twitchy all day."

"Twitchy?"

"You jump every time someone drives up the road."

A jolt of fear that she was being so transparent raced through her. "I was watching for the plumber and the electrician. And I'm expecting a delivery." She had to get away from him before she started babbling like an idiot.

He released his grip, and for a moment she wasn't sure she was glad. But then she regained her common sense and moved toward the debris pile again. Brady pitched in and helped carry the rest of the unusable materials to the barrel. Talk about twitchy. Being around him made her feel more on edge than watching for the feds to show up on her doorstep. Something about the intensity of his eyes and the powerful physicality of him made her hyperaware of his every movement. She so didn't need to be feeling that way about a guy.

She'd caught herself watching him on occasion today, how the muscles in his arms flexed as he sawed lumber, how much power was behind his strikes of the hammer, how the sweat soaked through his white T-shirt.

She eyed the creek and nearly took a flying leap into it to cool herself off. As if the early-summer heat wasn't enough, her temporary carpenter had to increase her body temperature even more. Maybe she'd find her sanity again when he went back to Kingsport and his real job.

When he dumped the last of the accumulated debris in the barrel, she glanced up at him and tried to convince herself that he wasn't a well-built, gorgeous man who made her wonder what he looked like without that dirty, sweaty T-shirt.

"Thanks," she said before lowering her gaze again. Good grief, if she didn't get away from him soon she was going to embarrass herself by drooling.

So desperate was she for a distraction that she didn't even remember to be nervous when she heard a vehicle coming up the lane. Thankfully, it revealed itself as the UPS guy with her expected delivery—the wildflower-ringed dishes for the café.

Audrey shooed Brady back inside to help his dad as

she took care of hauling the delivered boxes upstairs for storage until the lower level was totally finished. A couple of times, she caught Brady glancing at her as she went up the stairs. Only he wasn't looking at her as if he was searching for signs of an asthma attack. She got the impression he was watching her legs. Her face heated even more at that thought, so after carrying the last box upstairs, she flopped down on her bed and stared at the ceiling.

Why was simply being near Brady affecting her this way, making her all jittery? She barely knew the guy. She couldn't remember ever feeling this strangely around Darren, and she'd thought she would spend the rest of her life with him. Was it only a physical, hormonal thing? Brady was bigger, masculine and very, very sexy. Darren had been attractive and capable of getting her blood pumping, but there was just some-thing…*more* about Brady. Maybe she was just enjoying the sexy-carpenter fantasy. After all, she'd never heard of a sexy-stockbroker fantasy.

Especially not a stockbroker who dumped the woman he supposedly loved because her tanking repu-tation might ruin his career.

Not wanting to go down that mental road, she sprang from the bed and walked to her desk. She pulled her checkbook from the drawer and, after running some numbers, wrote out checks to Nelson and Brady. To prove to herself that she could avoid any infatuated feelings about Brady, she deliberately didn't brush her work-messed hair before descending the stairs.

"I was beginning to think you fell asleep up there," Nelson said as he held a two-by-four in place for Brady to hammer.

"No, had to do a bit of paperwork." When she reached the bottom of the stairs, she extended the checks to them.

"What's this?" Nelson asked.

Audrey caught Brady's eye before looking away. "Payment for all the work you two have been doing."

"We're just being neighborly," Nelson said.

"Dropping off someone's mail or giving her a potted plant is neighborly. This," she said as she indicated the interior of the mill, "is a lot of work for which I insist on paying you."

"That's not necessary," Brady said, surprising her with the sincerity of his tone.

She caught his gaze again and held it this time. "It is if you want to continue helping. Who do you think I would have hired, anyway? I'm guessing there's only one construction company in town."

His eyes stayed locked on hers for a moment, then he nodded as he took the proffered check from her. She thought she saw respect in his expression, and that meant more to her than anything he'd done for her so far. Her heart swelled at the thought of that much-desired respect.

It meant so much that she forgot her decision to not think of Brady in a romantic way and smiled at him. When he smiled back, her heart somersaulted like it was trying out for the U.S. gymnastics team.

Afraid she might start giggling like a thirteen-year-old girl, she glanced over at Nelson, who unfortunately looked like he was trying to hide a smile himself. Fantastic. He'd probably caught the goofball look on her face and knew his son was the cause of it.

"It's been a long day," she said. "Why don't you two pack it in for the evening."

"On one condition," Nelson said.

Wary, she examined his expression. "And that would be?"

"You let us make you dinner."

She nearly laughed at the stricken, openmouthed expression on Brady's face as he shot a look at his dad. She might have declined otherwise, but that look sealed the deal. This had disaster in the making written all over it, but in a hilarious way. She couldn't resist seeing what these two came up with. They could always drive into Willow Glen or even Elizabethton if the culinary results were inedible.

"It's a deal. What time?"

"Six-thirty," Nelson said as he wiped his hands on the towel that always hung from his belt.

"See you then."

From the shady area inside the doorway, Audrey watched father and son drive away and couldn't help the excitement pulsing in her, even if this dinner might be a bad idea.

*It's just dinner with two friends,* she told herself. Yeah, but one of those friends was extremely easy on the eyes.

# Chapter Five

"What are you up to?" Brady asked his dad as he drove down the lane away from the mill.

"Up to?" Nelson feigned innocence, but Brady wasn't fooled.

"Yes, up to. I swear I saw the little devil walking along your shoulder back there."

Nelson snorted on the passenger side of the truck. "I'm just inviting a friend over for dinner."

"Uh-huh."

"What is it you think I'm up to?" His dad pinned him with a probing look that made Brady glad he had to keep his eyes on the road ahead.

"I think you've let Sophie's matchmaker instinct rub off on you."

"Well, now, that's not a bad idea," Nelson said, as if the idea hadn't already occurred to him.

"I'm not getting involved with Audrey, so you can put that idea out of your head right now."

"Why not? She's a nice girl."

"Because."

"She's not Ginny." Nelson's words were kind but firm.

"I know that."

His dad didn't respond, but Brady could imagine all the things going through his head. How Brady needed to let Ginny's betrayal go, find a good woman and settle down. Easier said than done if you were always wondering whether dates wanted you or your bank account.

"I'm just too busy to get involved with anyone." His dad ought to know that, with the Kingsport office barely two months old.

"So busy that you're over at her place every day, stealing glances at her every chance you get."

"I'm here to spend time with you, and you happen to be spending your time over there." Brady didn't look at his father because his dad had always been good at seeing what his children weren't saying.

"And the glances part?"

"You're seeing things, old man." Irritation colored Brady's words as he pulled into his dad's driveway.

"Yeah, I'm seeing my son appreciate a beautiful young woman."

Brady hazarded a look at his father as he shoved the truck into Park and turned off the ignition. "Audrey and I are just acquaintances, friends if you stretch it."

"That's how your mother and I started out."

Brady sighed. "We're not you and Mom."

"Not yet."

Fatigue weighed down on Brady. He didn't feel like belaboring this point anymore. With a shake of his head, he stepped out of the truck, leaving his dad behind, and went straight for the shower. He needed to clean up because he stank, not because he wanted to look good for Audrey when she arrived.

Right.

As he showered, he couldn't get rid of the memory of her long, tanned legs going up and down those stairs leading to the mill's loft. Those were the kind of legs that drove a man crazy with wanting.

He rubbed his hand over his face and wondered why he was fighting this so hard. Just because his first attempt at a long-term commitment had ended in disaster didn't mean he couldn't enjoy a woman's company. It hadn't stopped him before.

But this wasn't merely a casual acquaintance back in Kingsport. This was someone his dad was treating very much like a daughter, not someone Brady could have a little fun with and then leave. He turned off the water and stood dripping. The thing was, his normal couple-of-dates-and-out M.O. didn't feel right where Audrey was concerned. Something about her made him want to get to know her, really know her. Maybe that's what was so damned scary. Part of him did want what his parents had enjoyed. But when he'd thought he'd found it, he'd been burned. Finding out someone you loved was in love with someone else didn't do wonders for a guy's confidence in his romantic judgment.

Despite his determination to stay detached, he still fought the urge to dress nicer than normal for dinner. He growled in frustration as he pulled on a pair of clean but faded jeans and a fresh blue T-shirt instead. When he wandered into the kitchen, he noticed his dad had showered, as well, but he'd put on a pair of khaki pants and a button-up green shirt. He was standing over the counter reading one of Brady's mom's recipe cards.

Nelson glanced at him and rolled his eyes. "Nice to see you dressed up for company."

"I'm clean. That's better than the last time she saw me."

When the phone rang, Brady grabbed it to avoid further discussion about Audrey. "Hello."

"That's a nice tone to use to greet your sister," Sophie said from the other end of the line.

"Sorry." No need to bite her head off.

"What's up with you?"

"Nothing." He leaned against the wall.

"Mmm-hmm," she said, obviously not believing him. "So, I hear you two are having dinner with Audrey tonight. And I hear she's pretty. You should totally go for her."

Brady sighed. "Dad put you up to this, didn't he?"

"Oh, don't sound so ganged up on. So what if he did? You know I want you to find the perfect girl. Maybe you'd be less grumpy."

"I'm not grumpy."

"Yeah, right. You're a riot of fun and frivolity."

Brady pushed away from the wall and stared at the phone as if it were part of the conspiracy, too. "Did you have a *real* reason for calling?"

"What, teasing my big brother isn't reason enough?" When Brady didn't respond, she went on. "Okay, fine.

Tell Dad that the girls are wanting to come visit and to call me when he has a free day."

After Brady agreed to relay the message, he hung up.

His dad sighed as he shook his head and consulted a recipe card. Whether his frustration was caused by the recipe or Brady's attitude, Brady didn't know.

"Melt a stick of butter," Nelson said.

"Dad, why don't we just take Audrey out to dinner? It'd be easier."

"Because I want to eat here. I want to eat one of your mother's best dishes." Nelson paused for a moment. "Because I want to hear a woman's voice in this house again."

Brady swallowed hard at the pain and need he heard in his father's voice. Nelson had been doing so well lately that Brady had almost forgotten he was still in mourning. Maybe Audrey had been right. It was hardest for his dad at night, when he had to go home alone and face the house he'd shared with his wife for forty years.

Brady walked to the refrigerator and pulled out the butter.

By the time six-thirty rolled around, the two of them had fumbled their way through making chicken-and-rice casserole, green beans, corn-bread muffins and an orange bundt cake. They wouldn't have their own Food Network show anytime soon, but Brady surveyed the results and figured they were at least edible.

When he heard the sound of an engine in the driveway, followed by a car door shutting, he deliberately took his time refilling the napkin holder on the table before heading to the front door. He wouldn't give his dad the satisfaction of witnessing how anxious he was to see Audrey again. Even if he had to admit he was.

She knocked before he left the kitchen, and he didn't hurry on his way to the door. Despite his attempts to be casual, he nearly swallowed his tongue when he saw her. She'd showered, too, and he'd swear he could smell flowers when he opened the door. Maybe that was the sensation a person experienced when his brain was short-circuiting. She wore a pink, sleeveless top and a white pair of those too-short pants.

"Hello?" Audrey waved her hand in front of his face.

"Oh, sorry. Mind was somewhere else." He opened the door wider to let her in.

"I'll say. You looked like you'd gone off to a galaxy far, far away and forgot to take your body with you."

"Work stuff," he said as he noticed her toes peeking out of the ends of her white canvas sandals. The toenail polish matched her pink shirt. He'd never thought toes were sexy, but hers were. She was right. His brain had taken off for regions unknown.

Only when she raised her hands did he realize she held a bowl.

"I made a salad."

He took the bowl from her. "You didn't have to do that."

She followed him inside as he backed out of the way. "I have a rule. Never arrive to dinner at someone's house without bringing something to add to the meal."

Now that he thought about it, he couldn't imagine Ginny having such a rule.

"You're just in time," Nelson said as he walked out of the kitchen and opened his arms wide.

When Audrey stepped into the brief hug, a surge of jealousy shot through Brady. How sad was that? Jealous of his dad's easiness with her. He walked past them, set the salad on the table and started scrounging in drawers to find that big spoon and fork his mom had always used for salads.

"They're in the drawer beneath the microwave." His dad led Audrey into the kitchen.

When he found them and turned around, he nearly bumped into Audrey. His breath caught as he got a whiff of some flowery scent. His imagination shot to her in the shower, lathering her hair with shampoo.

She looked up at him. "Is something wrong?"

"No." He jerked himself out of that daydream and moved past her toward the table.

"Could have fooled me," she said under her breath.

He needed to cool it. He'd determined not to act too interested in her, but he didn't have to be rude in the process. He had to find a middle-of-the-road reaction and stick to it.

"I hope you're hungry," Nelson said.

Audrey moved toward the chair Nelson had pulled out for her. "Starved."

Brady couldn't help thinking he was starved, too, and not only for the food on the table. Something besides his stomach was gnawing at him to be fed.

*Focus on the food, focus on the food.*

He did exactly that as they passed the dishes around. His dad carried the weight of the conversation.

"I think a couple more days and we'll be finished with our part of the kitchen, and you can arrange to have all the appliances brought in once the wiring is finished."

"You two have been doing a great job. I really appreciate it. I wouldn't be so far along without your help."

"I couldn't visualize the place as a restaurant at first, but I'm beginning to see the potential," Brady said.

Audrey smiled at him, and this time he yearned to cover that smile with his lips. That smile could get any man to do anything for her. She lit up the whole room. Stick some wings on her and she'd pass for an angel. Was it sacrilegious to think of her as angelic and sexy at the same time?

"I can't tell you how excited about it I am," she said as she placed a corn muffin on her plate. "I keep getting so many ideas that it feels like my brain is going to explode sometimes."

"I think your place is just what Willow Glen needs, a burst of something new." Nelson punctuated the word *new* with a short thrust of his fork.

Audrey smiled at him before taking a bite of the casserole. "Mmm, this is wonderful."

Brady's dad beamed. "It was my Betty's recipe."

It was the first time since his mom's stroke that he'd seen his dad speak her name with a smile. If for nothing else, he had Audrey to thank for that.

"Then she was a fantastic cook."

"That she was." A hint of the familiar sadness attached itself to Nelson's words when he had to refer to his wife in the past tense.

Brady watched as Audrey steered his dad away from his sorrow by asking about all the other dishes they had prepared. He wondered if her experience helping out after Hurricane Katrina had molded her ability to pick people up after tragedy or if she possessed some innate talent.

Brady stayed quiet while he listened to Audrey and his dad talk. For some strange reason, it struck him that maybe Nelson's friendship meant as much to Audrey as hers did to his dad. Brady couldn't pinpoint why that feeling was so strong, but it didn't fade as the evening passed.

"Oh, no, you made cake, too," Audrey said when Nelson pulled the bundt from under its lid on the countertop. She placed her hand on her stomach. "I think you're trying to fatten me up."

"You've been working so much, a little cake isn't going to hurt your figure. Let's just hope it's edible. Brady made it."

Audrey eyed Brady with mischief glinting in her blue eyes. "Was there an Easy-Bake Oven in your past?"

Nelson snorted, nearly choking on his cup of coffee.

"Oh, sorry." Audrey reached to aid his dad.

Nelson waved her away. "No, no, I'm fine. I only wish Sophie was here."

"Dad," Brady said in a warning voice.

Audrey looked between the two of them. "What am I missing? I'm sensing a good story here."

"It's nothing."

Nelson started laughing.

"That doesn't sound like nothing," Audrey said. "Come on, spill."

"Just that Brady does have a bit of Easy-Bake experience. Seems I remember him helping Sophie make about a dozen little cakes for the family one Christmas."

"She was sick!" Brady rolled his eyes. "This is the story that won't go away." He directed his attention to Audrey. "Sophie got the oven for her birthday, and she was determined to make everyone in the family a little cake for Christmas. But she got sick."

"And you offered to help her?" She said it in that tone that said there was an "awwww" behind her words.

"She asked me to, and I said I would only help if she swore not to tell anyone I'd been anywhere near that oven."

"Obviously, that didn't work out." Audrey pressed her lips together, like she was trying to keep from smiling.

"No, the little blabbermouth told anyone who'd listen."

Audrey snickered. "That's cute. Did you wear an apron?"

Brady sat back in his chair. "Ha-ha, very funny."

Nelson slid thick slices of cake in front of Audrey and Brady. "There's nothing wrong with a man knowing how to cook. I should have paid more attention the past forty years."

Audrey patted Nelson's hand. "You did a great job with dinner. It's much better than anything I could have pulled out of my cooler." She pulled her hand back and sliced off a bite of cake with her fork. "I'm looking forward to having a refrigerator and stove again."

Brady pictured her standing in the kitchen he and his father were building. He figured it'd be full of light and flowers, maybe a touch of mischief, just like Audrey's personality.

"This is good, too," she said after swallowing the first bite of cake. "I'd say the Easy-Bake lessons paid off."

"Okay, that's it." Brady balled up his napkin and pitched it at her.

She squealed, then laughed as she picked up the napkin and hurled it back at him. "Maybe I should pay you in aprons and Betty Crocker cake mixes, eh?"

He was searching for a suitable retort when the back door opened and in walked Craig.

"Hey, why didn't I get invited to the party?" He walked in and play-punched Nelson's shoulder as he had countless times before.

When his eyes lit on Audrey, appreciation and an I'm-so-available smile spread across his face. Brady's jaw clenched.

"Hello, I don't believe we've met. I'm Craig Williams."

Audrey shook his hand and glanced at Brady. "Ah, Brady's partner." She put the slightest inflection on *partner* again, then actually had the audacity to wink at Brady. She was enjoying this way too much. This called for retribution, if only he could think of some way to get her back that didn't involve trapping her against a wall and kissing her senseless.

She returned her attention to Craig. "You don't bake by any chance, do you?"

Nelson barked out a laugh, which caused Audrey to

lose her composure. Brady even had to smother a chuckle when he noticed Craig looking really confused.

Brady survived another recounting of the Easy-Bake Christmas tale by threatening to spread the story of Craig's blind date on his twenty-first birthday if he ever breathed a word to anyone.

"Oh, I sense another embarrassing story. Do tell." Audrey rubbed her palms together in anticipation.

"No, sirree," Craig said. "That story is never to be spoken aloud again."

Brady snorted. For years, the two of them had played one practical joke after another on each other, each time trying to outdo the other person's last joke. On Craig's twenty-first birthday, Brady had arranged for a "really hot" blind date to meet Craig at a Knoxville restaurant near the University of Tennessee campus where they were students. Brady had gotten a table in a corner to watch his best friend's reaction when he arrived and figured out his date was actually a cross-dressing man. He'd nearly fallen out of his chair laughing when realization hit Craig.

When they all finished their cake, they talked for a while about the work on the mill. Audrey's cell phone rang, and she excused herself to take the call in another room. Nelson put the dirty dishes in the sink then sauntered down the hallway to go to the bathroom.

"So, your dad seems to be doing better," Craig said.

"Yeah, staying busy is good for him."

"Sounds like you're staying busy, too. Does that mean you're getting busy, as well?" Craig nodded toward the doorway through which Audrey had disappeared.

"No. We're just helping her out. She's on her own."

"Such a shame for someone as pretty as her to be living the solo life. Maybe I should offer to keep her company."

"No." Brady bit down at the harsh sound of his answer.

Craig eyed Brady. "Uh-huh, I thought so."

"Thought what?"

"You like her."

Brady got up, stalked to the sink and started to run some water for the dishes. "She's a nice person."

"Who happens to be smokin' hot."

Brady eyed his friend and groaned in exasperation. "Do you think you could keep it down?"

"Dude, make a move before someone else does." Craig got up from his chair and smacked Brady on the side of the head on his way to the door. "Call me when you've gone over the figures," he said as he pointed at the manila folder he'd tossed onto the counter on his way in earlier.

Brady didn't respond to either command. He should focus on the figures for the construction bid, but instead he turned off the water so he might hear Audrey's voice.

When he did, she didn't sound happy.

"How DID YOU GET this number?" Audrey's pulse raced as she gripped the cell phone, the one with a new number, to her ear.

"It's pretty easy to track things like phone numbers, Miss York."

"I don't want to talk to you. Please don't call me again."

She pushed a button to end the call and stood shaking

in Nelson's living room. The reporter's voice still buzzed in her head, filling her with dread.

"You okay?"

She jumped at the sound of Brady's voice, her nerves frazzled. "Uh, yeah. I'm fine."

He walked toward her, his eyes narrowed and his face full of concern. "You sure? You look upset."

"Peachy." She waved the hand that held the cell phone and tried to force a carefree smile. From the unchanged look on his face, she didn't fool him. She glanced down, unable to stare into his probing eyes. "Just one of those uncomfortable family things."

"Want to talk about it?" He sounded awkward asking the question, like he wasn't used to doing so.

She appreciated the offer, especially from a man like Brady who didn't seem like the overly gabby type. But the last thing on earth she wanted to do was talk to him about her past and how it refused to leave her alone. She liked Brady, and spilling the whole messy truth would likely end their budding friendship.

"Nah. Actually, I'd better get going. Another busy day tomorrow."

"I'll walk you out."

"That's not necessary." She was afraid she was going to crack to pieces from trying to keep her shaking under control, and she didn't want that to happen in front of the guy who was occupying way too many of her thoughts. He'd even started invading her dreams the last couple of nights. She was surprised she was able to talk to him face-to-face after some of those dreams.

"I know." He followed her outside anyway, into one of those nights when the moon was so full and bright that you didn't need any other light to see by.

When she reached her car, she looked up and found him a little closer than she expected. Her breath caught in her throat for a moment. "Thanks for dinner. Tell your dad I had a nice time." She felt rude for leaving without saying goodbye herself, but she had to get away so she could drop the shaky facade of everything being fine.

"I will." He took a step forward, coming so close she'd swear she could feel the warmth coming off his body. "Are you positive you're okay?"

She let out a slow breath, then looked up at him and offered a small smile. "I will be." For a crazy moment, she considered leaning in and kissing him. Who could blame her? The man was more delicious than his orange cake, and they were standing here under a full moon with the crickets chirping and the cool evening air caressing them. And wouldn't it feel wonderful to be held and not ache from always being so alone?

But it was a bad idea, no matter how tempting it sounded.

He looked like he might be having similar thoughts as he eyed her mouth, so she opened her door and positioned it between them. "I'll see you in the morning."

Before she caved in to her desires and weaknesses, she got inside the car, started the engine and backed away from Brady. When she started down the road, she glanced in the rearview mirror. He stood bathed in moonlight, watching her leave.

Why did everything, including driving away from her carpenter, have to be so incredibly hard?

BRADY STOOD OUTSIDE until Audrey's headlights faded around the curve down the road. She might say she was okay, but he didn't believe it. That phone call had upset her, and when he'd looked into her eyes he'd seen fear. He'd seen the same look the day of her asthma attack, when she'd been about to fall backward at the park.

At the time, he'd assumed it had been because she couldn't breathe. But what if it had been something more? Had she seen something that had freaked her out? He couldn't imagine what, but the urge to stand between her and whatever might be threatening her rushed through him. He clenched his fists.

"Audrey left?" his dad asked from the front door.

"Yeah."

"What did you say?"

Brady turned and gave his dad an exasperated look. "Nothing. She said she had a full day tomorrow and needed to get home. She wanted me to tell you thanks for dinner."

"I would have made her up a plate to take with her."

"I think she can take care of herself, Dad."

And if she couldn't, he had the distinct feeling he would step into the void.

## Chapter Six

Audrey buried herself in work, even more so than she had in recent weeks. She helped Nelson and Brady with as much as she could, arranged for the delivery of everything she'd need to open for business, and made countless trips to Elizabethton to buy supplies.

At night, she continued to crunch numbers and investigate ways to invest what little savings she was going to have left so she could have an emergency cushion in case this dream of hers failed and she had to start over yet again somewhere else.

She hated the idea of leaving Willow Glen. As she cleared a path through the forest that would become the spur to the Willow Trail, she swallowed hard. She'd come to consider Nelson a much-missed father figure. This mill and slice of Appalachia felt more like home than her place in Nashville ever had, even though she'd lived there far longer.

And Brady... She couldn't deny she lit up inside every morning when she saw him. She fantasized about taking their relationship beyond the friendship that was growing every day, but it was too dangerous. She'd rather stay his friend and not have him find out about her past than risk never seeing him again.

Of course, he'd be going back home to his real job soon. He couldn't stay here as her carpenter forever. Still, she might run into him now and again in Willow Glen. Maybe she could invite him and Nelson over for dinner from time to time. She preferred to have him smile at her on those occasions than turn the other way in disgust.

"Hey."

She yelped and spun around, her leaf rake raised.

"Whoa," Brady said and held up his hand. "Do you always threaten guys bearing cold water?"

Embarrassment flooded her face as she propped the rake against a tree and tried to slow her pounding pulse. "Sorry. You startled me."

Brady walked closer and held out a water jug. She realized how parched she was when she heard the ice slosh against the inside of the container.

"You need to slow down," he said. "Your face is really red."

Yeah, because she'd almost whacked him with a leaf rake. "I'm okay. It's the fair skin, makes me look like a tomato if I do the least little thing."

He stepped closer, forcing her to look up at him.

"That's it. You're not doing 'the least little thing.' You're going nonstop, and if you don't slow down I'm going to be forced to tie you to a chair."

Her mouth dropped open.

"You heard me right," he said. "I know you want to get this place open, and I know something else is bothering you. But you're going to keel over if you don't stop once in a while and at least drink some water and cool down."

As if to prove his point, a wave of dizziness hit her and she reached for a tree trunk to steady herself.

Brady grabbed her hand and led her to a fallen tree a few feet away. "Sit before you fall down. And drink, slowly."

She did as she was told though in truth she wanted to gulp the water down as fast as she could. He was right. She was going to drop if she didn't slow down. Maybe she could relax a little. Hadn't it been nearly a week since she'd seen the newspaper article, and no one had shown up to question her yet again about her mother's finances? She'd been in the clear other than one more call from the reporter that she'd promptly erased without listening to it.

Brady sat beside her. "You seem to have forgotten your recent trip to the hospital. Why are you pushing yourself so hard?"

She shrugged, too tired to come up with some sort of excuse and not wanting to outright lie.

"We're making good progress. You can afford to dial it back."

She nodded and took another slow drink of water. The fear that she might lose everything again ate at her. It drove her to work to the point of exhaustion, hoping she'd be rewarded with being able to keep her new life intact.

Brady leaned toward her. "It's going to be okay." She glanced over and found his face close to hers, so close that the least movement forward on her part would bring them into some interesting territory. She heard him suck in a breath. But when she saw too much understanding in his eyes, she looked away. He knew she was hiding something from him.

She gripped the water jug more tightly to keep from shaking, from giving in to the insane urge to tell him everything to see how he'd react.

When he reached over and wrapped her hand in his much larger one, she took her turn at inhaling sharply. She closed her eyes and soaked in the feel of his warm skin against hers, wished she could stop worrying that someday he would walk out of her life as quickly as he'd come into it. Stop being concerned that it would matter.

"Whatever it is, it'll be okay." Brady squeezed her hand then got up and walked back toward the mill.

Audrey brought her hand, the one he'd held, up to her heart. How could she be falling for a man she barely knew?

She lowered her hand and looked at her palm, as if his touch had changed her in some profound way, and shook her head. When had common sense and the emotions of the heart ever followed the same path?

BRADY WATCHED Audrey for the next couple of days, trying to figure out what it was about her that made him so curious. While she didn't resume her frantic work pace, she still didn't take a lot of breaks, either. She had one heck of a work ethic, even if it was going to fry her at some point.

As he sat at his dad's kitchen table late one night, working on some plans for another project he and Craig were bidding on, his thoughts kept veering to Audrey and how single-minded she was in getting her new business off the ground. Almost as though if she didn't get it done by some unnamed date, it'd be the end of the world. Maybe she was running low on funds and needed the inflow of income. He could certainly understand that, though he still believed she needed to slow down. He tamped down the old suspicion about her motives when it tried to make a reappearance. She'd given him no reason to suspect she was after his money.

He shook his head and ran his fingers through his hair. His gut told him that whatever was bothering her was more than cash flow.

"What's got your forehead all scrunched up?" his dad asked from the doorway to the living room.

Brady closed the folder in front of him and slid it to the side of the table. "Just tired. I feel like my eyeballs are on fire."

"I think it's time we all took a day off. Think I'll stay here and fiddle with some furniture designs tomorrow, watch a little baseball."

"Maybe I'll sleep all day." Between the schedule he'd fallen into at Audrey's and his own work at night, he was beginning to feel like overcooked toast.

"Going to be another pretty day. You should go do something fun with Audrey."

Brady let out a slow sigh. "Dad. We've been over this."

"I heard what you said, but I've got eyes. Yours don't say what your mouth does."

Brady was too tired to argue. Instead, he got up from the table and headed to bed. Once in his boyhood room, however, he sat on the side of his bed and stared at the floor. What the hell? Maybe his dad was right. He could use a day off, and Audrey sure could the way she'd been working ever since he'd met her. He tried not to think about how much his mood improved once he'd made the decision to spend the day with her, alone and nowhere near a hammer. The big obstacle was convincing her.

KNOWING AUDREY WAS typically up and at work at the crack of dawn, Brady drove into the clearing as the first hints of pink were lightening the sky. He wasn't surprised that Audrey was already dressed when she stepped out onto the porch.

"What are you doing here so early?" she asked when he stepped out of his truck. "And what's with the canoe?"

"You and I are going for a ride down the creek today," he said as he walked toward her.

She shook her head and said, "I have too much—"

He stopped her objection by putting his index finger against her lips. His heart kicked up a notch at the feel of that softness against his skin. Her eyes widened in response. "No arguments. Even workaholics take a day off now and then. We both could use the break." How could he sound so practical and matter-of-fact when he wanted to replace his finger with his own lips? When he was freaking out at how Audrey made him feel, all antsy and overheated?

He lowered his hand and watched as she considered his words. He imagined the war going on inside her head—her natural instinct to spend every waking hour working versus the allure of playing hooky.

"Fine, but I want to get my camera." She spun and disappeared into the mill before he could process his shock that she'd caved so easily. He'd been prepared for a long argument and was surprised by how much he was determined to win it.

He decided not to analyze that too closely as he turned to unload his dad's canoe.

Once he had the canoe situated at the edge of the creek and loaded with the paddles and the cooler of food and drinks he'd brought, he straightened to find Audrey striding toward him with a camera bag over her shoulder. An unexpected bout of nervousness hit him. Would they find enough to talk about during their trip? He wasn't a huge talker, but at the moment he felt like he had absolutely nothing of interest to say. He questioned the outing it was now too late to back out of.

She glanced up through the trees. "I hate to waste a nice day for working. It's supposed to rain tomorrow."

Brady tried to ignore the stab of disappointment that she considered this trip a waste of time. Of course, she probably hadn't meant it that way. He was being too sensitive. Sophie would fall all over herself laughing if she knew how he was acting and thinking.

He had to think of today as a mental-health break for

both of them, nothing more. They'd been working long hours without a day off.

After she seated herself in the canoe, he shoved it into the flow of the creek and jumped in. He took up a paddle as she pulled her camera from its bag and placed it near her feet. She seemed ill at ease and fidgety as she grabbed her own paddle.

"Is something wrong?"

She glanced over her shoulder at him for only a moment. "No, just lots on my mind."

"That never-ending to-do list?"

She hesitated, long enough for him not to believe her when she said, "Yeah."

"It'll get done."

She fell into silence and he let her. She turned around and started paddling again. He imagined he felt the tension knotted up in her shoulders and fantasized about massaging it away, making her forget all the things that were preventing her from relaxing. Would she moan in pleasure, pushing him to the brink of control? He looked away, wondering how his self-assertion that this trip was nothing more than a break from work had disappeared so quickly.

After a few minutes of only the sound of the creek's flow and the birds overhead, she pointed toward the bank on the right. "Can we pull up over there?"

He steered them to the bank and held the canoe steady as she scampered out with her camera. When she squatted next to a pink wildflower of some sort, he realized she wanted to take some photos. Hey, if that would make her enjoy the day more, he'd turn the canoe into the Wildflower Express.

After she shot the flower from various angles and distances, she made her way back into the canoe. He started to hold out his hand for her, but she hopped in unassisted. Why did he feel cheated?

Brady nodded toward the flower. "Tell me if you want to stop again."

For the first time that morning, she really looked at him. "Thanks. I probably will want to photograph some more. I plan to put lots of native wildflower pictures in those frames your dad made and hang them all over the café."

He scrambled for another question to keep the conversation going. "You do lots of photography?"

She shrugged. "When I can. I really like it, but I haven't had much time the past few years." Her words held an edge of sadness.

"Well, there's plenty to take pictures of around here."

Audrey offered him a small smile as he climbed in the canoe. "I'm sorry if I've been a grump. Guess I'm a little stressed."

"Understandable. Can't say I've been without stress lately, either."

"You?"

"Yeah, Craig and I are bidding on several projects. It's kind of make-or-break time for the new location."

"Then why are you here? Shouldn't you be working?" She sounded guilty, like they should cut their trip short immediately.

"I have been."

"When, after you leave my place at night?"

He shrugged. "Yeah. Lots of it is paperwork and talking to people on the phone, stuff I can do from here. Plus, Craig and Kelly are holding the fort."

"Kelly?"

"Our intern."

"Oh."

Brady stared at Audrey's back. Had he heard what he thought he had? She'd almost sounded jealous.

He shook his head and made another stroke in the water. He was losing his mind.

They spent the morning talking about the work on the mill and her plans, safe topics. Every few minutes, Audrey would spot another type of flower and ask Brady to guide the canoe to the bank. Each time he did so, he saw a bit more of her tension fade. After taking several shots of a white flower she called a Rue Anemone, she even gave him a big smile.

"Those are going to be some awesome shots. The light was perfect."

"Why do I suddenly feel like I'm on *National Geographic Explorer?*"

She laughed. "I guess this wasn't what you had in mind for a leisurely float down the creek."

"It's fine. I'm glad to not be working today." He gestured toward the side of his head. "I was beginning to dream about trips to Lowe's."

"I hope you at least had an unlimited shopping spree in the dream."

"Hmm, that sounds more like a dream a woman would have, except to someplace other than Lowe's."

"Are you kidding? I'd love to win a big fat shopping spree there right about now."

Brady pictured her directing Lowe's employees out of the store with new kitchen appliances, lighting fixtures and lumber to build the gazebo.

A couple of minutes later, he spotted a sandbar in the middle of the creek, one shaded by the overhanging trees. "You hungry?"

"Actually, yeah."

He steered the canoe up on the sandbar. "Then welcome to the Sandbar Café, the best in midstream dining."

She chuckled at his fake maitre d' accent. "Why, thank you. I've heard this place is all the rage."

As they ate the cold-cut sandwiches and chips, Brady found himself watching Audrey's mouth and wondering how it would feel to kiss her. The animal instinct side of him threatened to leap across the canoe and kiss her. He'd never had that kind of reaction to a woman before—not even Ginny. It was exciting and scary at the same time.

Though she seemed to be in a better mood and more relaxed now than earlier, he still sensed that she was holding something back. He fought his instinct to suspect a hidden agenda. After all, why wouldn't she keep things to herself? It wasn't as if they were best buddies or lovers and all into sharing deep, dark secrets.

After they finished eating, Audrey stepped out onto the sandbar and stretched. Brady swallowed hard when that movement caused her T-shirt to ride up and reveal part of her flat stomach.

He readjusted himself on his seat and eyed the surface of the creek. No cold shower presented itself, but the creek would suffice. He stood up and shucked his shirt.

Audrey noticed his action and turned toward him. "What are you doing?"

"Going for a little swim." He jumped into the creek and let himself sink.

AUDREY'S HEART THUDDED against her breastbone when Brady broke the surface of the water, lifted his arm and rubbed his hand back over his hair as he found his footing on the creek bottom. Her mouth ironically went dry as she stared at the expanse of his wet torso. She'd always had an appreciation for a nicely toned male chest, and Brady's was right up there at the top of the list.

His eyes caught hers, and for the life of her she couldn't look away.

"Come on in," he said. "Feels good." He looked up toward the sun. "Today's going to be a hot one."

Going to be? Her skin was already so hot she feared she'd make the creek boil if she stepped into the water.

"I didn't wear a bathing suit."

"Don't need one."

She swallowed hard.

"Was that a naughty thought that went through your head?" His smile stretched wide, flustering her.

"No. I just don't want to get my clothes wet."

"Why? They'll dry quickly today." He dialed back

the teasing, as if he'd been surprised he'd engaged in it in the first place.

She eyed the water, imagined how cool it'd feel against her overheated skin. An uncharacteristic urge to ignore common sense overcame her. She realized she'd decided to take the leap, so to speak, when she slipped off her athletic shoes and walked to the water lapping at the sandbar. As if he sensed her nervousness, Brady took a few steps back to give her room.

The cold of the water made her jump when she edged in the first few steps, but it also felt good as Brady had said it would. She did her best not to look at his wet chest, but she failed miserably. But if she gave in to the desire to run her hands up that chest, she would die of embarrassment. Then she'd run into the forest and hide until he went away.

"It's easier if you dive in, get it over with," Brady said.

"Huh?" Had he figured out what she was thinking?

He pointed toward the surface of the water. "The cold. Just dive under and you'll get used to it quicker."

"Oh."

He lifted an eyebrow. "You okay?"

"Yeah, fine." Unable to stand his scrutiny any longer, she took a breath, held her nose and submerged. When she came back up, she inhaled and squeezed the water from her ponytail.

"Better?"

"Yes." Of course, she hadn't looked at his chest again. Man, she felt like one enormous hormone. Sure, it'd been months since she'd been with a man, actually more than a year, but giving in to her current desire was a disaster waiting to pounce. No matter how much her body was badgering her to explore just a little.

Brady lowered his body into the water and swam around to the other side of her, cutting off any possible retreat to the canoe. "Audrey, you seriously need to lighten up. You're wound so tight, you're going to pop."

"No, I'm not." Of course, how her voice rose in defense negated her words.

And Brady knew it. He shook his head. Before she realized what he was up to, he swam toward her, grabbed her hand and pulled her farther into the water so that she had to swim.

"Hey!" She swatted at him as he swam away. "What was that for?"

"Your own good." He smiled, scrambling her brain again.

Oh, that's the way it was going to be, was it? She narrowed her eyes at him then dived in his direction. He evidently hadn't expected it, because his late attempt to get out of the way failed. Audrey took the advantage and pushed him under before trying to make a quick getaway.

*Trying,* that was the operative word.

Brady resurfaced in a matter of moments and dunked her in turn.

She came up sputtering. "Oh, you're in for it now."

"Yeah, I'm scared." He laughed, making her more determined to get the upper hand.

They circled each other, and when she couldn't find an opportunity to strike she splashed water in his direction instead. This only made him laugh more. Instead of biding her time, she let that laughter get to her and she made a dive for him. This time he moved out of the way and grabbed her on her way down.

Audrey stiffened as she realized how close he held her, his firm chest pressing against her soaked shirt. She caught his gaze, and neither of them averted their eyes. *Move away, move away,* her brain screamed at her. But she couldn't. She didn't want to. She wanted exactly what she knew was about to happen, and her eyes drifted shut a breath before Brady's warm, wet lips touched hers.

She moaned as he wrapped his arms more firmly around her and pulled her closer. Her whole body tensed in the most delicious way, and she slid her arms around his neck as he deepened the kiss.

Oh, it'd been so long since she'd felt this kind of thrumming awareness and need. A fantasy of making love on the sandbar flitted through her mind before the movement of Brady's hands on her back dashed the ability to think.

"Is this okay?" he whispered against her lips, his breath making them tingle.

"Mmm-hmm." She moved so that she could feel more of him.

He needed no further encouragement and delved into another kiss, his hand holding her head.

She kissed him back with a crazy need she only now realized she'd been keeping caged since she met him. She didn't really believe in love at first sight, but lust?

That was another matter altogether. Was she capable of having a purely physical relationship?

She didn't know, but right now she was willing to try.

When Brady broke the kiss to breathe, he pressed his forehead to hers. "I've been wanting to do that for a while."

"Really?" she said, sounding out of breath.

"Yeah. Don't sound so surprised. You'd make a saint melt," he said with a voice gone husky with desire.

She blushed then initiated another quick kiss. "You're not hard on the eyes, either." Or the mouth.

Brady cradled her face in his big hands. "Then I should have dunked you in the creek sooner." He cut off her response with yet another mind-disabling kiss before growling and pulling away.

"What's wrong?"

"As much as I'd like to continue this, we're supposed to meet Dad at the takeout point in about an hour. If we're late, we'll never hear the end of it."

Audrey tried not to let her disappointment, or her arousal, show as they stole a few more kisses before getting back in the canoe and heading downstream. Maybe if they got back to the mill before the headiness of the kissing wore off, they could send Nelson home and indulge in a little more.

Her thoughts went to her bed in the mill's attic, and she wondered if she could go through with sex for sex's sake. She pushed away thoughts of wanting more, of how she was opening herself up to pain again. If Brady found out about her mother and looked at her differently, if he pulled away, could she bear to stay at the mill he'd helped her refurbish?

When Brady stopped paddling, she turned to see what was wrong. He surprised her by being so close.

"I wanted another one of these before we reach the old man." He took her face in his hands again and kissed her like they were facing the end of time. When he pulled away, he chuckled at what must be an addled expression on her face.

As they rounded a bend in the creek and she spotted Nelson's pickup, she fought to wipe her silly grin away. Even if she and Brady couldn't continue what they'd started this afternoon, she was pretty sure she was going to have some hot dreams tonight.

She buried her smile when they floated a little farther downstream and she noticed Nelson wasn't alone. He stood next to his truck while a blond woman and two little blond girls sat swinging their legs on the tailgate.

"Who are they?" she asked Brady under her breath.

"My sister and nieces."

"Oh." Was their presence a good or bad thing? Disappointment that getting rid of Nelson just got a lot harder flowed through her.

"Uncle Brady!" the little girls squealed in unison and waved with enthusiasm.

"Hey, rugrats."

"About time you two got here," Nelson said in fake exasperation as they pulled up to the gravel takeout point. "A man could grow old waiting."

"You're already old," Brady said as he stepped out

of the canoe and pulled it farther out of the water so Audrey could step out.

Nelson grabbed the ever-present towel hanging from his belt and snapped it against Brady's arm. Audrey smiled to see the teasing between father and son, a good sign that maybe they were beginning to heal from their recent loss. They'd no doubt have bad days ahead, but at least bright spots made appearances, too.

Just like today in her life. She'd been so afraid of the past catching up to her that she'd forgotten she should be enjoying the present. Wasn't that what moving to Willow Glen and reimagining the mill was all about, starting a new, better life? Maybe she needed to take a few chances outside of the leap of faith regarding her new business.

"You must be Audrey," Brady's sister said as she approached her and offered her hand. "I'm Sophie. And these two," she said as she pointed to where her daughters had wrapped their arms around their uncle's legs, "are Annie and Bethany."

Audrey shook Sophie's hand and noticed how much she looked like her brother, but in a lovely, feminine way where Brady was all hunky male. "Nice to meet you. Sorry to have kept Brady from his uncle duties."

Sophie made a dismissive gesture with her hand. "No need to apologize. If he spoils these two any more, I won't be able to stand living with them."

Still, as Audrey watched Brady and Nelson load the canoe, she wanted to make some gesture of friendship to these newly met members of the Witt family.

"Do you all have dinner plans?" she asked.

"Nothing yet," Sophie said. "Figure we'll whip up something at Dad's before we head back to Asheville."

"Can I interest you in letting me use all of you as guinea pigs?" She scanned the entire group, an almost-complete family, something she hadn't had in years. She blinked before her longing could cause tears to form.

Brady looked back at her with a hungry expression that had her cheeks flaming again and an intensity that said he wished everyone but Audrey would disappear.

"What do you have in mind?" Sophie asked.

Audrey redirected her gaze to the other woman so she didn't have to see the frustration on Brady's face. "I need to try out some of the recipes I plan to use in the restaurant, make sure someone besides me likes them."

"Sounds good to me," Brady said.

What was he up to? She was certain food was the furthest thing from his mind. Was he hoping to feed everyone then ship them back to his dad's house so they could be alone?

"Now that answer was too quick," Nelson said. "I think my boy doesn't like my cooking."

"Pork and beans were fine the first three times we had them," Brady threw back.

"Oh, get in the truck before I leave your ungrateful carcass here and make you walk home."

"A meal I don't have to cook," Sophie said. "I'm so there. I need to run by Dad's first, then we'll be over to help out."

"Oh, there's no need."

Sophie wrapped her arm around Audrey's as they

walked up the embankment. "Of course there is. I've got to know more about the woman who got my big brother to take a day off from work."

Audrey started to argue that it wasn't like that, but she caught sight of the mirth on Brady's face and the words caught in her throat. Was it like that?

"See you all in a few minutes," Sophie said as she rounded up her girls and ushered them into her car.

"Hope you're ready to be grilled to within an inch of your life," Brady said as he stepped up next to Audrey.

"Can I plead the fifth?"

Brady laughed then slid into the middle of the bench seat, leaving the space next to the window for Audrey.

On the way back to the mill, Brady kept looking over at her and giving her looks that promised more excellent kissing. From where his arm lay along the back of the seat, he played with her ponytail, causing her nerves to sizzle like lit fuses. Finally, she mouthed, "Stop it!" He smiled wide in response. When she'd met him, she would have never guessed this side of the man existed. Maybe it took a while for him to warm up to people.

Speaking of warm, her skin heated every time a bump in the road caused their legs to rub together. She closed her eyes and looked out her window when those sensations made her imagine their legs entwined and rubbing along each other in a soft bed.

Even with the aching thoughts and sexual frustration, she wouldn't trade today for anything. She hadn't enjoyed herself so much in a long time, had forgotten what it felt like.

She should have known it wouldn't last.

## Chapter Seven

"Looks like you've got some company," Nelson said as he drove within view of the mill.

A man sat on her front porch, and a silver car was parked in the shade nearby. She didn't recognize him, but she didn't have to. Her hammering heart rate told her it wasn't anyone she wanted to see.

Out of the corner of her eye, she noticed Brady look from the man to her. "You know him?" he asked.

Audrey tried to quell her rising panic and sound casual. "No." She didn't elaborate, afraid her voice would break. She needed to get Nelson and Brady out of here before this stranger said something to ruin everything. Despite her care, she felt Brady tense.

When Nelson came to a stop, she slid out of the truck and headed straight for the man. She forced a friendly smile she was far from feeling. "Hello, can I help you?"

The man stood, his khakis and golf shirt contrasting with her shorts and tee. "Yes, I'm Joe Spellman. We've spoken before."

The reporter. The bastard didn't take no for an answer. Her panic ratcheted up another notch.

She spoke, interrupting him before he said any more. "Oh, yes, if you'll give me a few minutes, we'll talk." Again, before he could respond, she spun and walked toward Nelson and Brady to keep them from coming any closer. She felt her fake smile threaten to crack as she turned her back to Spellman.

Brady saw her distress and took a few steps toward her. "What's wrong?"

"Nothing. I've just got to take care of some business. How about we plan that dinner for tomorrow night instead?"

Brady stepped closer and lowered his voice. "I can stay."

"No need."

He glanced past her toward Spellman before capturing her gaze. "I saw how that guy being here affected you when we drove up. You didn't want to see him. I'm not leaving you here alone."

She glanced to where Nelson was also eyeing Spellman, then edged back a step. "You're overreacting. He isn't here to hurt me." Not physically, anyway.

"Who is he?"

"Nobody. Really, you two go on home. Tell Sophie we'll reschedule the dinner."

He looked like he was going to argue again, so she took one of his hands between hers. "I'm fine, I swear. I'll see you in the morning."

Brady shot what could only be called a warning look

over her shoulder toward Spellman. It might have annoyed her at some points during her life, but right now it warmed her to have someone care about her even a little. But she had to get him out of here before Spellman destroyed what might be the start of something.

Her common sense tried to intrude, telling her that there could never be anything more than what she currently had with Brady. If she went further, she'd have to tell him about who she was. And she couldn't envision that turning out well.

"Will it help if I promise to call if I need you?"

Brady still didn't look happy about leaving, but he nodded.

"Are you sure?" Nelson asked from the other side of his truck.

"Yes." *Please, just go before Spellman opens his mouth again.*

For a moment, she thought Brady might kiss her. Part of her so wanted that kiss, but she couldn't allow that to happen in front of the reporter. She didn't want Brady touched by whatever Spellman had in mind. Instead of moving in for a kiss, however, Brady squeezed her hand then headed for his own truck. She didn't move until he followed his father down the lane and out of sight.

"Looks like you've made some friends here already," Spellman said from behind her.

She took a deep, slow breath before facing him, but it didn't help. Her nerves were still firing like a string of firecrackers. "What do you want?"

"An interview."

"No."

"Hear me out." He advanced a few steps toward her.

She maneuvered past him to situate herself next to the porch. If he became too much of a problem, she could go inside and lock him out. "You people made my life hell for months. What makes you think I'd cooperate now?"

He looked confused. "Didn't you get my message?"

"I erased it."

"What I said was that I wanted to tell your side of the story."

She pointed toward herself. "My *side* of the story is the truth."

"Then let's tell people that."

She shook her head. "I tried that already. Didn't work out so well." She sighed. "I just want to get on with my life. I don't want to relive this over and over."

Spellman exhaled and paced for a moment. "I thought with the change in the situation you might want to speak out."

"You mean the fact investigators are looking to possibly make more arrests and you want to be there for the scoop because you think it's me?"

He frowned as if she'd lost her mind. "No. I'm talking about your mom's condition."

"Condition?"

"Yeah, the breast cancer diagnosis."

Audrey's head spun, and she sat down hard on the edge of the porch. Cancer? Of all the reasons she'd thought this man had shown up in her new life, this scenario had never even entered her mind.

Spellman kneeled in front of her. "Are you okay?"

God, no, she wasn't okay. Her mother, the woman she'd pushed out of her life, had cancer. She felt the first hint of wheezing in her lungs but fought to calm herself. Having an asthma attack in front of this man, leaving herself vulnerable, was not an option.

She let her head fall forward into her hands and stared at the ground. Bile burned the back of her throat, and the sandwiches from the Sandbar Café threatened to make an unwanted reappearance. She heard movement, but it didn't register what Spellman was doing until he returned from his car and extended a bottle of water to her. With shaky hands, she took it, wishing it were something much stronger. Something that would make the world go away and cause Spellman's words to reveal themselves as lies.

Audrey downed half the bottle before meeting Spellman's eyes.

He shifted from one foot to the other. "I'm sorry. I figured you knew."

She stared hard at him. "Why would you assume that?"

"Because she's your mother." His gentle tone irritated her. Like he cared about her or her mother beyond the story they could provide him.

"And I haven't talked to her in months," Audrey said, her voice rising. "If you'd done your homework, you'd know that. What my mother did ruined my life. I had to start over, and now you're here to ruin this one."

"I'm not." His words were calm and sounded genuine, but Audrey ignored that fact because she wanted to be mad at him, at the entire situation.

"Most people would have taken the clue when I didn't call back that I didn't want to talk."

Spellman slid his hands into his pants pockets. "I may be a journalist, but I'm the first to admit there's a pack mentality in my profession. This is what I do, go through past coverage and try to figure out what angle hasn't been covered."

"And you figured you'd show up and shock me into saying something that would get a juicy headline and you a front-page byline."

He tilted his head slightly. "You always think the worst of people?" He didn't sound accusatory, merely curious.

"I didn't used to." Once upon a time, she'd sought out the good in everyone. She'd believed in the work her mother's ministry was doing—wonderful social and economic projects to help the world's poor, both in the U.S. and abroad. Some of it had been real; she'd seen it with her own eyes. But there'd been lies, too, lies that still tore her apart when she allowed herself to think of them.

Her insides twisted. The old anger toward her mother tugged at her from one side while worry about her mother's health pulled at the other. She didn't know how to feel.

Spellman sat at the edge of the porch. "I've talked to your mother several times. She's a good woman."

She narrowed her eyes at him, wondering if this was part of his disarming technique to get interviewees to open up. "Good people don't steal from others."

"She knows what she did was wrong, and she's sorry. For hurting you most of all."

Audrey sat stunned by the revelation for several heartbeats, wondering how well he knew her mother. "She should have thought of that before she bilked people out of money so she could live her cushy lifestyle."

Spellman clasped his hands together and let them hang between his knees. "All I'm saying is that I don't believe the situation is all black and white. There's a significant amount of gray." He slid a card from his pocket and placed it on the porch between them. "I only wanted to speak to you in person, but I won't push anymore. If you ever change your mind and find you want to talk, give me a call."

She sat stone-still as he walked to his car, got in and drove away. Hoping to escape the maelstrom raging inside her, she stood on shaky legs and walked toward the creek, followed it away from the mill into the forest. As if the heavens felt the need to match her mood, the forecasted rain arrived early. She paid it no heed, letting her clothes get soaked for the second time today. Thinking back to the earlier reason, she stopped and propped her hand against the rough bark of a tree. She let memories of the wonderful hours she'd spent canoeing with Brady push aside some of her sorrow for a moment.

As insane as it sounded, she was dangerously close to falling for Brady Witt, and falling hard. Those beautiful emotions tangled with the anger that her mother's actions had made her life so difficult and the new fear that she might very well lose the only parent she had left.

Even if she hadn't talked to her mom in months, at least she'd known she was still out there, still breathing.

Audrey propped her forehead against the tree and let her mind rove back over memories of her mom, good ones. Thomasina tucking her in at night and reading her bedtime stories. The time they'd gone to Disney World and her mom had ridden "It's a Small World" with her at least a dozen times. The way she'd made chocolate-chip pancakes for Audrey's birthday every year until she'd gone to college.

She pulled back her hand and slapped her palm against the tree, then again, and again, over and over. The rain started to fall harder as she let out an anguished cry, dropped to her knees and let the sobs come.

BRADY DROVE into the clearing next to the mill, glad to see the unknown man's silver car was gone. Still, as he stepped out into the rain and didn't see Audrey, something felt wrong. He'd been a fool to leave her despite her assurances that all was okay. She'd been upset by the man's appearance. Anyone could have seen that. Was this man what she'd been running from? When she'd watched the lane to the mill with anxiety tightening her expression, had she been afraid this man would show up?

Brady shoved down images of Shawn Bennett, the man Ginny had kept hidden from him, the one she'd plotted with to get Brady's money.

Even with those thoughts plaguing him, he was still worried about Audrey. Why had he relented and left as she asked? But he'd only been able to stay at his dad's house about twenty minutes, ones in which he'd paced and worried, before he'd said to hell with it and driven back here.

But the area was too quiet now. Sure, the rain was pattering against the leaves in the trees and the tin roof of the mill, but the absence of any sound caused by Audrey had him hurrying toward the front door. Halfway there, he heard a cry from the wooded area on his left.

Audrey. Fear shot through him like a lightning bolt.

He'd kill the bastard if he'd hurt her. He raced toward the sound of her cries, his heart beating faster with each stride. He found her on her knees next to a tree, bent low and crying. She jumped and her eyes rounded when he slid to his knees beside her.

"It's okay. It's just me." He ran his hands over her hair, down her arms, checking for injury, desperate to find the hurt and make it go away. "What did he do to you? I swear I'll kill him."

Audrey shook her head. "He didn't do anything."

Brady didn't believe her. "He had to. You're in the middle of the woods crying your eyes out."

She lifted a shaky hand to wipe at her cheeks then stared toward the creek. A deep, mournful sigh escaped her, making her appear as if she was going to crumple. Watching her like this made him ache with helplessness.

"What is it?"

She looked down to where she clasped her hands tightly together. "My mom is ill. She has cancer."

"Oh, honey, I'm so sorry." He pulled her into his

arms, and the chill from her body soaked into him. "Come on, we need to get you inside. You're freezing."

She didn't balk, but simply let him guide her to the mill. Once inside, he sat her on one of the benches along the wall and took off her socks and shoes. "You need to go change."

Audrey stood, zombielike, took two steps before stopping. "Come with me."

At first he thought it was her distress talking, that she didn't think she could make it up the stairs. But then their eyes met and he grasped her meaning.

"I don't want to be alone."

Though it pained him, he shook his head. "I don't think now is the best time."

A tear trickled out of her eye, and that undid him. He walked forward and took her into his arms again, telling himself he would help her upstairs then leave her to undress alone. She clung to him as if desperate for the warmth and comfort he could offer, and he knew he'd give it to her. He was a weak, weak man. Audrey didn't let go as he guided her up the creaking wooden stairs to her living area. His eyes found the bed first, and he couldn't stop his body's reaction to the thought of lying in it with her.

Her thoughts were running along the same track as she clasped his hand and led him toward the bed. When she reached down and pulled her shirt over her head, his breath caught as if it had forgotten the way out of his lungs.

"Audrey."

"Shh." She lifted to her toes and placed her mouth on his.

The kiss went from a touch to deep hunger in a flash and, heaven help him, he gave in. He was a man with a half-naked, soaking-wet woman in his arms, after all. Even the sound of the rain on the tin roof faded as the rest of their clothes went flying in all directions and they wrapped themselves together under the covers.

AUDREY WOKE SLOWLY and snuggled deeper into the covers. Before she opened her eyes, she noticed that the rain had stopped. How long had she been asleep?

She opened her eyes and noticed the sun filtering into her room—but at the wrong angle. Had she slept all night? That wasn't possible. She slid up and sat at the head of the bed, pulling the covers with her since she was still naked. Everything came back to her—Spellman's revelation, her conflicted feelings toward her mother, the way Brady had made love to her and then held her close without asking questions. She had fallen asleep, and she remembered the feeling as she'd drifted off. Contentment, safety, happiness.

Another glance around the room convinced her that the impossible had indeed occurred. She'd slept through the night, something she hadn't done in more than a year.

She looked over to where the other side of the bed was still rumpled and missed Brady's presence there. Feeling about sixteen, she slid back down in the bed and smelled the pillow Brady had used. With her eyes closed, she inhaled deeply. It smelled like a mixture of rain, fabric softener and that indefinable male scent of his. She hugged the pillow close as she remembered how tender he'd been with her but also energetic at all the right times.

Where was he now?

A loud noise from downstairs made her jump and her heart race. Then came a muttered oath and what sounded like a dropped frying pan. Pushing all the worries from the day before away for the moment, she slid out of bed and into her bathrobe.

When she opened the door at the top of the stairs, the scent of frying bacon met her. She peeked into the main level to make sure Nelson wasn't there, as well. When she didn't see him, she made her way down the stairs and to the doorway to the kitchen at the bottom. Brady stood inside the recently completed kitchen picking up what looked like the remains of cooked eggs with a paper towel. He still wore the cargo shorts and T-shirt from the day before and no shoes.

"Have an accident?"

He looked up at her, and the frustration on his face faded and was replaced by a satisfied grin. "Good morning."

"Apparently." She indicated the sun shining through the windows.

"Sorry I woke you."

"I think I slept long enough. Sorry I conked out like that."

He tossed the paper towel in the trash can then closed the distance between them. "You have nothing to apologize for. You had a long, rough day."

She didn't want to think about that now. Later, but not now. She met his gaze. Warmth stole over her, tempting her to take another day off. This time they could spend it in bed talking, laughing, loving. "It ended very nicely, though."

Brady moved closer and enclosed her in his arms. "Can't argue with that." He lowered his mouth to hers, dissolving her with another kiss. As if she'd been doing it her entire life, she stepped toward him and wrapped her arms around his neck and kissed him with all the happiness whirling inside her. She'd deal with the bad stuff later. For now, she couldn't pull herself away from how wonderful it felt to be held by him.

Heat followed Brady's hands as he ran them up her back, much as that same heat had the night before. His breath next to her ear made her want him all over again.

"I made you breakfast, but it's supposed to be breakfast in bed. So no food for you until you're back under the covers."

She smiled against his throat. "Nice line. It work well for you?"

He leaned back and looked her in the eyes. "I don't know. I've never used it before."

"Well, then, I'd better get your track record off to a good start." She stepped away from him and jogged back up the stairs. When she reached the second level, a wave of guilt hit her. How could she be enjoying herself like this when her mother was battling cancer?

Brady's footsteps on the stairs urged her to hurry to the bed. She stuffed her legs under the covers as he stepped into the large, open room.

In the absence of a tray and the real dishes that were

still packed in boxes in the corner of her living space, he'd placed the paper plate filled with scrambled eggs, bacon and toast on a square of plywood. "It's not fancy, but I'm fairly sure it's edible."

She smiled as she ripped open a plasticware set that had come with one of the many takeout meals she'd had since arriving in Willow Glen. "It's certainly more than my usual half a bagel. Thank you."

Brady slid into bed with her and nabbed a piece of her bacon.

"Hey."

"Cook's prerogative."

The food was good, but with each bite Audrey's heart ached a little more. Last night had been wonderful and this morning a dream, but it wasn't real, not lasting. It couldn't be unless she came clean with him about who she was and what her life had been like before she came to Willow Glen. The thought spoiled her appetite and she pushed away her breakfast though she'd only eaten about half of it.

"Something wrong with the food?" He sounded so concerned that it only added to her aching.

Audrey shook her head. "No, it's fine. It's just…"

Brady took the makeshift tray and placed it on the floor next to his side of the bed. Then he wrapped his arm around her and pulled her close. "Take your time."

She did. In fact, she lay with her head against his chest, listening to the rhythm of his heartbeat, for what seemed like hours. One moment she'd be on the verge of spilling everything, the next she'd talk herself out of it, convinced she couldn't stand losing Brady when she'd only found him.

When Brady leaned over and kissed the top of her head, it broke the trance she'd been in. She moved out of the warm circle of his arm and sat facing him, her legs crossed and her eyes staring at the sheet.

"I feel guilty about enjoying this time with you."

"Because of your mom?"

"Yes, but for more reasons than you know."

"You said you weren't close."

She fidgeted, picking at her cuticles. "We used to be, though, until a little more than a year ago."

"What happened?"

Audrey took a shaky breath, wondering if she could go through with this. But she needed to know how he'd react. Because however he took the news would likely be how the other residents of Willow Glen would receive her identity, as well. And if this place and this new life weren't going to work out, she needed to know now before she got any more invested in it—financially or emotionally.

So nervous she couldn't sit still, she got up and paced the floor.

"You can tell me," Brady said. "I know everyone isn't close to their parents. I'm not going to think less of you."

She stopped pacing and met his gaze. "I hope not. But we'll see." After a few more anxious steps, she stopped again and sank onto a cushy chair on the opposite side of the loft from the bed. "I used to work for my mother, enjoyed it and believed in my job." She twisted her hands, wondering if she could go on.

"But something happened and you had a falling out."

"You could say that." She inhaled deeply then let it out before plunging forward. "My mother is Thomasina York."

At first, the name didn't seem to register with him. She watched, waited, knew the moment her mother's identity clicked in his mind. His eyes widened and he shifted on the bed.

"The TV preacher who was sent to prison?"

Audrey swallowed past the growing lump in her throat. It felt like she was trying to swallow a lemon whole. "Yes."

"And you worked for her?"

"Yes. I was a fund-raiser."

Brady was quiet for interminable seconds in which Audrey wanted to run away and not have to rip the rest of the story out of herself.

"Were you involved?"

Audrey fought her rising nausea and the edge of panic making it more difficult to breathe. "Not in the fraud, though it didn't matter in the end. Everyone looked at me as if I was guilty anyway."

"That's why you came here, to start over?"

She nodded. "I couldn't get a job. My friends didn't want to be my friends anymore. I couldn't go anywhere or do anything without suspicion following me around like a dark cloud."

Brady got out of the bed and walked to the window at the end of the loft. He braced his arms against the wall on either side and stared outside. "Who was that guy yesterday?"

"A reporter. He'd been calling and leaving me messages, but I erased them without listening."

"He the one who called you that night at Dad's?"

"Yes. The press nearly ate me alive after Mom's arrest, me and everyone else who worked for my mother's ministry because they believed in the good work we were doing."

"Good work? I wouldn't call embezzling good work. It could have been my parents' money. They have always given to church projects."

Audrey looked up at the ceiling to prevent the tears in her eyes from falling. "We were all fully investigated. Yes, I was stupid not to ask more questions about my mother's lifestyle, but I honestly didn't know." She returned her gaze to him. "Brady, the ministry did fund a lot of good programs—women's shelters, food pantries, schools and medical clinics in war-torn countries. I know. I saw them with my own eyes. I helped build homes and schools and medical clinics with my own hands."

"But not all of the money went to those things."

"No, it didn't." She lowered her head and looked at the pattern on the large area rug she'd placed on the wood-plank floor. Out of the corner of her eye, she noticed Brady turn toward her.

"So what did the reporter want if you were cleared and your mother's already been sent to prison?"

"A new angle. Me to tell my side of the story."

"They haven't already covered that?" He sounded as if he couldn't believe the media had overlooked such an obvious viewpoint.

Her stomach swirled. She placed her hand against it as if that would calm her nerves. "They weren't very interested. They'd already made up their minds I had to be guilty."

Brady walked the several steps back to the end of the bed and sat facing her. He looked like he was struggling with something, but at least he wasn't walking away. He looked down at the floor. "Sounds like it was tough on you."

"It was." Her voice cracked. "I was hurt, embarrassed, felt like a fool."

Brady met her eyes, and the overwhelming need to tell him everything pressed against the inside of her heart, begging to be released.

"My dad was a pastor of a church outside Nashville, and he was a wonderful man. He did lots of work with Habitat for Humanity, the homeless mission in Nashville, basically anything that could help those less fortunate. But he worked too hard." She swallowed painfully when the image of her father's last moments came back to her.

"We always ate lunch together, just him, Mom and me, every Sunday after church. He'd take us somewhere different every week. He said it was his treat for Mom, who'd cooked all week. When I was ten, we'd just started eating lunch one Sunday in a new restaurant when…" She sniffed against the tears. "Dad clutched his chest and fell over right there in front of me and Mom. He died of a heart attack before the ambulance could get there."

"I'm sorry."

Audrey nodded that she'd heard Brady's sympathy, but she couldn't stop now. She had to get it all out before it ate any more of her soul.

"Mom had always been very active in church as the minister's wife, but now she felt she had to do the work of two people. She threw herself into church work in addition to getting a job as a secretary. Eventually, she started her own congregation and gave up the secretary job. The congregation grew and grew, was eventually broadcast on the local TV station, grew some more. By the time I was in high school, she was being broadcast nationwide and able to fund all kinds of social projects. I believed in her so much that after I got out of college, I started working as a fund-raiser for the ministry. She moved to Colorado to start a new headquarters, but I stayed behind because Nashville was my home. I had friends, a place of my own, contacts all through the Southeast."

She stopped and sucked in a breath. "When I heard my mom was being investigated for fraud, for taking some of the funds and using them for her own purposes, I didn't believe it. I thought it was some enemy out to muddy her good name. But then the investigators showed me the proof. I thought I would die right there, sitting across the table from them."

The memories sliced at her and made her want crawl into a corner and cry. But she'd shed so many tears already because of what her mother had done. They'd been part of her daily life as every last inch of her privacy had been exposed to the world.

"As if learning my mother had done those things wasn't bad enough, I had to endure an investigation into my possible involvement. And even though I was cleared of any wrongdoing, my life as I'd known it was basically over. I'd lost everything—even the man I thought I'd marry."

"You were engaged?" Brady's voice sounded strained as he asked the question.

Audrey clenched her hands until her knuckles went white. "No, but things were headed that way. Turns out he wanted his upward mobility more than me. I went from the woman he said he loved to a liability. He didn't even have the decency to tell me to my face. He mailed my things to me with a note that it wasn't going to work out between us."

The unwanted tears finally won the battle and trickled down her face. She swiped at them, directing her anger and hurt at those twin tracks of water.

Brady surprised her when he slid off the bed, came to kneel in front of her and took her into his arms. Starved for emotional and physical comfort, she dissolved against him. She really let go and allowed the tears to flow freely. She wanted to stay there in his arms forever so he could keep the world at bay. She didn't like being weak, but it proved hard to be strong all the time.

"Shh," he said next to her ear.

After a few more moments, she got herself under control and sat back. "I'm sorry."

He wiped at a stray tear with his thumb. "Sounds like you went through a lot."

"You know, when I first saw you and your dad together, it made my heart ache. I admit I was jealous, still am sometimes." She looked up into his eyes. "I can't tell you how betrayed I felt by my mom. And now…now I don't know how to feel. I've not gotten over being angry at her, but she's still my mom."

"And she's sick."

"Yeah." She brushed away a tear. "How can I feel furious and guilty at the same time?"

Brady shook his head. "Feelings are messed-up things sometimes."

"Tell me about it." She glanced at the bed behind him. "I'm sorry I didn't tell you…before." *Before we had sex and I was in danger of losing my heart to you.*

He took her hand and squeezed it. "Don't worry about that. I probably wouldn't have told anyone, either."

Did she dare hope he was going to be okay with everything she'd revealed to him, or would he start thinking of ways to distance himself the first time he was out of her sight?

"Can I give you some unsolicited advice?" he asked.

She shrugged.

"Maybe it's time to talk to your mom."

Audrey knew he was thinking of his own mother and how he'd never be able to talk to her again, but things weren't that simple. She'd said some awful things to her mom, words meant to hurt her as much as Audrey had been hurt. And she couldn't pretend her mother hadn't done anything wrong.

"I don't know."

"Just think about it. Going to see her doesn't mean you have to forget everything else."

Audrey wrapped her hands around Brady's. "I was so nervous about telling you."

"I'm glad you did." There was something in his expression, concern maybe. Audrey didn't try too hard to identify it, afraid of what she might see.

She offered a shaky smile and wished he'd kiss her, suffuse her with that feeling of euphoria he had the day before. When he didn't make a move to do so, she bit her lip and tried not to read anything into it.

Maybe he was right, that she should go see her mother. If she didn't and the worst happened, would she regret it for the rest of her life? But if she left, would her time away give Brady the opportunity to really think about the situation and choose his professional reputation over a relationship with her like Darren had? Could she blame him if he did? After all, they hadn't known each other anywhere near as long as she and Darren had.

Then why did this thing with Brady feel more real, making her relationship with Darren seem like a hollow shell?

Brady stood, bringing her with him. "You've got a lot to think about. I need to go before Dad sends out a search party." He gave her a small smile then a kiss on the cheek. "I'll see you later."

She nodded, then wrapped her arms around herself as she watched him leave the loft. She understood that

Nelson might be worried about him. She even missed that kind of concern about her own well-being. But it still felt like Brady was already pulling away, taking the first steps out of her life.

## Chapter Eight

Over the next couple of days, Audrey did a lot of thinking as she worked. The mill renovations were coming along really well, beginning to look like the café she had been dreaming about since that day standing in the magazine section of the bookstore. She should be happy now, but she wasn't.

Her feelings toward her mother were still twisted in knots, and she and Brady didn't share any more intimacy. He still worked at the mill during the day and smiled at her whenever their gazes met, but no more. Maybe he was giving her room and time to figure things out, not pushing her, but she couldn't help thinking he moved further away from her each day. Hadn't that been how her friends had drifted away? When the renovation was completed, would he simply disappear from her life?

She buried those thoughts in work, her normal means of escape. Her vision of the café was close enough to reality now that she could plan an opening date. She consulted the calendar, committed to July 1, just in time for the Independence Day weekend. Despite everything going on in her life, solidifying the date felt like a gigantic accomplishment. Something solid, real. Something she could control. To celebrate, she went into Johnson City and Elizabethton to arrange for newspaper ads announcing the grand opening.

When she returned to the mill, she found Nelson and Brady moving in the tables and chairs Nelson had built for the café. She sat in her car for a minute and soaked in the scene, enjoying how the dream was becoming reality.

At least the café part of her dream.

The tables made everything look different when she walked in. As she approached one, she noticed that Nelson had improvised on the plain surface design they'd agreed upon. One of her hands came to her mouth as she ran the fingers of the other over the carved and painted wildflowers around the edge of one table.

"These are beautiful," she said as Nelson came to stand beside her.

"The flowers were Brady's idea."

She shifted her gaze to Brady and found him standing off to the side looking uncharacteristically awkward as he shifted his weight from one foot to the other. Maybe she'd been worrying about his leaving for no reason, letting paranoia get the better of her. More likely, he'd suggested this design before he'd known about her mother's arrest and her own part in the aftermath.

"Thank you. I love them."

Brady smiled and nodded. It wasn't the type of smile

he'd given her after they kissed at the creek, but she'd take it over a frown any day.

After a morning of working with the guys who'd arrived to repair the waterwheel, Audrey stepped inside to where the new air-conditioning cooled her skin. She walked into the kitchen where Nelson and Brady were cleaning up the last of their carpentry mess. The gleam of the new appliances reminded her of the breakfast Brady had cooked for her using them. Then she remembered the meal she'd promised them several days before.

"I believe I owe you two a meal. How about tonight?"

Nelson leaned back against the counter. "Sounds good to me. We're about finished here and I've got to tend to some business in town, so I'll catch up with you two later."

With Nelson's departure, awkwardness invaded the kitchen.

"You don't have to cook for us," Brady said as he washed his hands then wiped them on a wad of paper towels.

"I want to. You and your dad have done so much for me, in so short a time." She edged closer to him. "I'll have to think of some special way to thank you for the tables."

"It was nothing." He shrugged. "Made sense if you're going to put those flower pictures on the walls."

She wanted him to wrap her in his arms, to kiss her as he had the night they'd made love. "Is something wrong?"

He shook his head. "No. Just a lot on my mind."

"About what I told you?"

"Partly. Other stuff, too."

Hoping she wasn't making a mistake, she lifted to her toes and planted a kiss on his cheek close to his mouth. As she'd hoped, he inhaled sharply and turned so that his lips met hers.

While it wasn't as passionate as before, she'd take it. At least he hadn't avoided the kiss.

Brady ended the kiss and took a step back.

She clamped down on her need to be reassured. With a shaky smile, she stepped back and shoved her hands into her pockets.

"I've got to run to Kingsport this afternoon," Brady said. "Craig and I are presenting a bid to a potential customer, and I need to get cleaned up."

"This the bid you've been working on at night?"

"Yeah." A half laugh accompanied a shake of his head.

"What?"

"Ironic that the bid is for a big church retreat."

Audrey suppressed the nervousness that shot through her, tried to act as if this news didn't affect her, didn't make her worry that Brady would still decide any contact with her was too risky. Instead, she offered him support. "Sounds like a good opportunity for your company. Good luck."

"Thanks." He gave her an intent look, as if trying to determine if she was serious. She held her breath until he nodded. "If we get the job, we'll have more to celebrate tonight."

"Right. I'm confident you'll get it, so I'll make something extra special."

He caught her gaze and smiled, really smiled this

time. Like he'd let go of whatever had been bothering him. A spark of the magic she'd felt between them a few nights before dissolved some of her fears.

"I'm looking forward to it," he said, then kissed her forehead before heading out the door.

Risking some teasing, she slid her cell phone out of her pocket and dialed Nelson's number.

"Hello?"

"Hey, I have a quick question."

"Shoot."

"What's Brady's favorite dessert?"

BRADY GLANCED AT THE CLOCK as the business meeting went longer than he'd anticipated. He'd have to fly low to make it back to Willow Glen in time for dinner at Audrey's. But this meeting wasn't something he could rush. Even though Witt Construction was a long-standing, successful business, the new location still had to prove itself. And that required big projects like Lakeview Christian Retreat.

He and Craig worked in tandem to lay out all the plans and figures they'd been working on during the past few weeks. Thankfully, the Lakeview developers seemed impressed.

"This all looks great," Harold McReynolds said as he nodded at the plans in front of him. "You boys have got yourself a deal."

A surge of excitement and pride shot through Brady. He couldn't wait to tell his dad. Audrey's face also swam through his mind. Concern about being duped again had caused him to pull back from her since she'd shared the story of who she was with him. But despite his own past, he believed everything she'd told him about herself was true. She'd proven herself over and over with her hard work and kindness to his family.

McReynolds insisted on a round of celebratory coffees, so by the time Brady was able to free himself he was obviously going to be late to dinner. Still, he hurried out the entrance to the restaurant and ran right into someone.

"Oh, I'm sorry," he said as he steadied the woman and took a step back. His eyes met Ginny's.

Seeing her again knocked the wind out of him. She was still beautiful with her coppery hair and bright green eyes, but revulsion marched side by side with the physical appreciation.

"Brady," she said, her widened eyes and fidgeting with her purse telling him her surprise ran as deep as his. "It's been a long time."

Not long enough. "Yes." He glanced at the man standing next to her in a possessive stance. It wasn't Shawn.

"Brady Witt, this is Cole Brandicott, my husband."

Brandicott looked as if his bank account fit his name and his expensive suit. Poor sucker. Brady bit down on the violent desire to spill everything he knew about Ginny and her gold-digging ways, but the desire to get away from her overrode the urge. Plus, he heard Craig approaching with the Lakeview guys behind him and had no desire to be forced to make introductions between Ginny and his new clients.

He nodded at Ginny's husband and said, "Excuse me. I'm late for an appointment." He didn't even meet Ginny's eyes again as he exited and headed for his truck. She didn't deserve one more moment of his time.

Despite his desire to get to Willow Glen, he didn't steer in that direction. Instead, he found himself following the series of streets that took him back to the office. Once in the parking lot, he turned off the truck's engine and stared at the dark building, then ran his hand over his face. Ever since he'd left Willow Glen earlier in the day, one thing and then another had conspired to keep him away. And what were the chances of running into Ginny in Kingsport? Last he'd heard, she had moved to Knoxville. And to see her tonight of all nights. It almost felt like a sign, a warning that he was in danger of following the same ill-advised path he had before.

He slammed the base of his palm against the steering wheel, then got out of the truck and stalked inside. What was the use of going back to Willow Glen now, anyway? He'd be really late, and he was in a foul mood. Not exactly great dinner company.

He stared at the phone and wished it would make the call for him.

AUDREY HAD SPENT her afternoon in a whirlwind. Tomorrow she'd likely make plans to visit her mother, but tonight she wanted to wrap herself in the beauty of this new life of hers. The café, her friendship with Nelson, the way her heart swelled when she thought of Brady.

Tonight she'd enjoy their company. Tomorrow she'd deal with the not-so-beautiful parts of her life.

She ran back and forth between the kitchen and her loft, alternating between preparing the special meal of salmon with lemon-pepper sauce, marinated baby vegetables and Asian spinach salad, and making herself look as nice as possible. To mark the beginning of what she'd decided to call the Willow Creek Café, she slipped into a filmy summer dress printed with wildflowers and a pair of pink sandals. Putting her hair up into a loose knot showed off her dangling pink earrings.

A quick glance at her clock had her zipping back downstairs to give the meal the final touches and set it on the table. Her heart rate quickened when she heard the truck pulling into the drive outside. Her smile faded, however, when she stepped out onto the porch and saw that Nelson was alone. To his credit, he'd brought her a multicolored bouquet of flowers that she recognized from the Glen Grocery.

"Why, thank you, kind sir," she said with forced happiness when he reached the porch and extended the bouquet to her.

"Pretty flowers for a pretty lady. I talked to Brady halfway through his meeting. He said he'd probably be running a little late and he'd join us here."

She relaxed as she led the way inside so she could put the flowers in water. She filled an old Mason jar she'd found in the loft then cut the flowers' stems to fit. With the arrangement in the middle of the table, everything looked perfect.

Nelson sat at the table and surveyed the room. "Everything looks great. I think it's going to be a big success."

"I certainly hope so. I couldn't have done it without you and Brady."

"It was nice to have something to do."

Audrey looked at Nelson's profile, saw that he was thinking about his wife again. "You miss her a lot, don't you?"

"Every moment of every day." He took a deep breath then let it out. "I think if I hadn't been able to work here, I might have lost my mind."

She reached over and squeezed his hand. "Then I'm glad I had loads for you to do."

He chuckled a little. "Betty would have liked you."

"I'm sure I would have liked her, as well."

"I think I know someone else who likes you, too."

Audrey blushed and pulled her hand back to her lap.

"And based on your call earlier, I'd say the feeling is mutual," Nelson said.

"I only wanted to do something nice to thank him for the flowers on the tables."

"Uh-huh."

She swatted at him. "Hey, since when is Cupid an old guy who wears Red Wing boots?"

"Who you calling old?"

She made a dramatic show of looking in every direction before her gaze landed on him again.

"You sure are a sassy thing."

"And you love it."

To keep the food warm until Brady arrived, Audrey

placed it in the oven. Then to pass the time, Nelson helped her hang the wildflower pictures around the room. When they hung the last one, of the Rue Anemone she'd shot during her canoe trip with Brady, tears filled her eyes.

"What's wrong, honey?"

She shook her head. "Nothing. I just can't believe it's really happening." She directed her hand around the room to indicate the realization of her dream.

If only all aspects of her life were as wonderful as this moment, she'd be able to breathe easily and be totally happy. But maybe she was being overly selfish and asking for too much.

That thought reverberated in her head more often as the minutes ticked by and Brady didn't arrive. The doubts about their budding relationship resurfaced, and it became harder and harder to ignore them.

When her cell phone rang, she hoped it was Brady saying he was almost there.

"Hey," he said when she answered.

"Hi. Are you getting close? I've kept the food warm."

"I'm sorry, but I'm not going to be able to make it. Our meeting ran long, and I've still got a lot of work to do."

Audrey's heart sank at the distance in his voice. "Oh, okay."

"Sorry to call so late."

"Don't worry about it," she said past the lump in her throat. "I understand."

She hated herself for doubting his words, but she'd been down this road before. Even so, she had a dear friend in her new home, a scrumptious meal she'd cooked and a lot of positive things to celebrate—even if some things in her life still threatened to shred her heart.

She ended the call and forced a smile in Nelson's direction. "Looks like it's just me and you tonight. Think you can handle dinner on your own with a sassy gal?"

For a moment she feared Nelson was going to ask her to elaborate on the call, but thankfully he simply grinned and said, "Sassy and the prettiest girl in Willow Glen."

Considering how she'd hoped the evening would go, Audrey had a better time than she expected. She and Nelson found lots to talk about, but as the conversation wound down she noticed him looking at her with sympathy in his eyes.

"Wow, I think my day is catching up with me," she said as she pushed herself to her feet. "If you don't mind, I'll send the dessert home with you." She hurried off to the kitchen before Nelson could say anything. Once a wall stood between her and Nelson, she let her fake smile drop away and gave herself a mental pep talk.

*You barely know Brady. So you had sex one time. What is that? Not exactly a promise of lifelong commitment. You knew the risk when you took it.*

She'd hold her emotions together until Nelson left. Then she'd have a good, long cry before pulling herself up by the proverbial bootstraps and getting on with her life—a new life that despite heartbreak held a lot of exciting possibilities.

With the lemon pie in her hands, she returned to the main room. "Maybe you two can dig in to this after Brady gets back."

"Audrey—"

She held up a hand. "There's no need to explain or apologize. I'm a big girl. Plus, we're the lucky ones. We got to enjoy our dinner instead of working all night, right?"

Nelson stepped forward and gave her a hug. "Thank you for dinner. Based on what my taste buds are saying, this place is going to be a huge success."

"Thanks." She planted a kiss on his cheek and kept the smile on her face until he drove away.

For the next few minutes, she cleared the table, washed the dishes, basically anything that could delay going upstairs. Being alone up there was worse than being alone down here. Soon she'd have customers filling this lower level, but when she went up to bed at night she would still be alone.

After finishing in the kitchen, she walked through the dining area, running her fingers over the carved flowers on the tables. She'd have to cover them with circular pieces of glass before opening, but for now she wanted to feel the evidence of Brady's thoughtfulness.

He wasn't a bad person, and part of her didn't blame him if he was having second thoughts about getting more involved with someone who came with so much baggage. Still, it hurt. It surprised her how much his actions caused her heart to ache, how quickly he'd come to mean a great deal to her.

When she couldn't put it off any longer, she climbed the stairs. The loft, however, felt cavernous and lonely. She sank into the chair and let her thoughts wander. As the minutes ticked away, she came to the conclusion that in order to go forward, whatever her future might hold, she had to make peace with the past. And that meant going to visit her mother.

She wouldn't sleep a wink tonight anyway, so she went to her closet, pulled out her suitcase and started packing. That completed, she called the airline.

"Yes, I need to book a flight for tomorrow morning, the earliest one you have from Nashville to Denver."

If she couldn't sleep tonight, she might as well spend the next several hours driving halfway across the state to catch a direct flight. Hours when she could think, hours to plan, hours to prepare herself for what awaited her in Denver—and when she returned to Willow Glen.

BRADY'S EYES BURNED as he stared at the blueprints spread out in front of him. The sound of the door opening startled him.

"What are you doing here?" Craig asked as he stepped inside. "Aren't you supposed to be having dinner with Audrey?"

"Change of plans." Brady returned his attention to the blueprints and realized he'd been staring at them for who knew how many minutes without even seeing them.

Craig stalked across the room until he was standing in front of Brady. "You're the biggest damn idiot I've ever met. You let seeing Ginny screw with your head, didn't you?"

"I just have work to do."

Craig cursed. "You have got to let your...baggage, or whatever the heck shrinks call it, go. So Ginny did a number on you. It's over. Move the hell on. Audrey isn't like Ginny."

Brady's fists clenched. "How do you know?"

"Because she doesn't have dollar signs flashing in her eyes. Come on, man, what are the odds you'd hook up with two money-hungry women in one lifetime? Besides, it's not like you're freaking Bill Gates or something. You ain't *that* rich."

The words sank in, past all the stupid doubts. His father and sister had said similar things to him over and over, but it took his best friend confronting him about his warped view on things to make it click.

"Besides," Craig said as he flopped in a cushy chair in the corner, "if you don't hurry up and get with this woman, I'm going to sweep her off her feet."

Brady narrowed his eyes at Craig before surging to his feet and toward the door. As he drove back to Willow Glen, he felt like he'd been up for three straight days. He hated that he'd talked himself into missing dinner with Audrey, but he hoped she'd forgive him and maybe invite him in for some leftovers.

And then, maybe, they could spend the rest of the night together. Just talking if that was what she needed. He rubbed his hand over his face, not quite able to believe how often he thought about her, how much he wanted to be near her when he wasn't.

The clock in his truck read 10:46 p.m. when he turned onto the lane leading to the mill. He probably should have waited until morning. Audrey might even be asleep. But the need to see her and apologize in person wouldn't loosen its grip on him. He didn't want her going to sleep tonight thinking the worst, that he was no better than all the other people who'd abandoned her.

He second-guessed himself, however, when he pulled into the clearing and saw that the mill sat dark. Damn. She'd been working so hard and now was facing a really difficult situation with her mother, so she needed as much rest as she could grab. Coming here so late had been selfish.

Hoping he hadn't ruined her sleep, he turned off his headlights as he circled around to leave. That's when he realized her Jetta wasn't there. He flicked the headlights back on. Where could she be? To be sure she really wasn't home, he slipped out of the truck and went to knock on the door. Nothing moved, and he heard no sounds other than the truck engine running. Audrey wasn't here.

She might be at his dad's house. He hurried back to his truck. His excitement died, however, when he pulled into his dad's driveway and saw no Jetta. Maybe his dad knew where she'd gone.

He found his dad in his recliner watching the eleven-o'clock news. Nelson looked up when Brady walked in the door then returned his attention to the TV as if he was disappointed in him.

"There's a lemon pie in the fridge if you want a slice."

"Lemon pie?"

"Yes, your favorite, remember?" Nelson's sarcasm cloaked each word. "Audrey made it for you."

She'd made his favorite dessert. How had she… She

must have asked his dad. His guilt for skipping dinner, for allowing doubt to stick its claws into him again, grew.

"Do you know where she is?"

"She called, said she had to go out of town for a few days. I assume it has something to do with her mother."

Brady walked to the center of the room. "She told you about her mom?"

"She didn't have to," Nelson said in a tone that told Brady he didn't give his dad enough credit. "I read the paper. I put two and two together."

"So you know?"

"That her mother is Thomasina York? Yes."

"And it doesn't bother you?"

Nelson clicked off the TV and met his son's gaze. "Why would it? Audrey isn't the one who stole the money."

"I know that." Brady sank onto the arm of a chair. "Her mom's sick. She's got cancer."

"Is that why that guy was there the other day?"

Brady's fists clenched. "No, he was a reporter looking for a story. But he's how she found out about her mom's illness."

"Damn." Nelson shook his head. "That poor girl."

And Brady had made everything even worse.

The need to hear Audrey's voice, to make sure she was okay, swamped Brady. He grabbed the cell phone from his belt and headed out the door. "I'll be back in a minute."

He dialed her cell and paced the front walkway until she answered.

"Audrey, are you okay?"

"Yeah," she said, sounding confused.

He relaxed some, glad to know that she was at least safe. "Where are you? I came by, but you weren't home."

"You did?" Surprise weaved itself around her simple question.

Guilt gnawed at him. Craig was right. He'd been an idiot.

"Yeah. I wanted to see you, to apologize for missing dinner."

He thought he heard a sniffle. "Audrey?"

"I'm fine, on my way to Nashville. I'm flying to Denver in the morning."

"To visit your mom?"

"Yeah."

He hesitated for a moment, unsure of the right thing to say. "Do you want me to come with you?"

Silence greeted him on the other end of the line, and he gritted his teeth. He had said the wrong thing. Damn, he'd done nothing but make bad decisions all day.

"That's sweet of you to offer, but I…I think this is something I need to face on my own."

Disappointment that he couldn't help her tugged at him. "Will you call if you need me, even if you just want to talk?"

"You surprise me, Brady Witt." He welcomed how her voice lightened.

"How?"

"I never pegged you for the type to give phone therapy sessions."

"Hey, even a guy like me can listen," he said, lightening his own tone to match hers. He leaned against the bumper of his truck and wondered if maybe she needed a little humor to get her through. "You know, there are other things we could talk about on the phone."

"Really? Do tell."

He lowered his voice. "So, what are you wearing?"

Her laughter lifted his mood. "Wouldn't you like to know?"

Brady couldn't help smiling then teasing her some more. In fact, he stood out beneath the stars and talked to her for more than an hour, until his cell-phone battery started to beep at him.

"Is that your girlfriend beeping in on the other line?" she asked.

"Nah, just another client calling in for a late-night session."

"Brady!"

He laughed and felt great that he'd helped improve her mood, that in some small way he'd begun to make up for his absence earlier. "Really, it's my dying cell battery. Call me when you get to Denver?"

"Sure."

"Good night, gorgeous."

"Good night, handsome."

Brady clicked the phone shut but stood outside a few minutes longer, until his stomach growled loud enough for the neighbors to hear and swear Bigfoot had taken up residence nearby. Time to raid the fridge.

His dad had already hit the hay by the time Brady stepped inside, so he tried not to make too much noise. He should really eat a sandwich or something substantial. But one look at the lemon pie with perfect meringue sitting on the top shelf of the refrigerator had him pulling it out and grabbing a knife and fork from the silverware drawer.

The first bite had him thinking he'd died and gone to dessert heaven. The pie was enough to make him fall the rest of the way in love with Audrey York.

Who was he kidding? Her cooking had nothing to do with the falling.

# Chapter Nine

The wet soles of Audrey's shoes squeaked on the floor of the hospital corridor as she walked from the elevator to the nurses' station at the end of the hall. The cold of the air-conditioning made her shiver. The quick rainstorm had caught her midway between her hotel and the hospital without an umbrella.

When she reached the nurses' station, a middle-aged nurse in daisy-print blue scrubs said, "Can I help you?"

"I'm looking for Thomasina York's room."

Audrey wasn't surprised to see the tightening around the nurse's mouth. "She's only allowed limited visitors. Are you family?"

Audrey met the woman's gaze and held it. "Her daughter."

There it was, that guilty-by-association look. To her credit, the nurse hid it better than most. Must be part of her training. After all, she probably had to hide her feelings a lot, what with having to sometimes treat people she didn't like.

She pulled a file out of a stand-up, metal file holder, opened it and consulted a paper inside.

"Your name?"

"Audrey York."

"You're on the prison-approved list," the nurse said with what sounded like suppressed disdain. "She's down the hall on the left, around the corner, Room 514. The one with the guard." That last part felt like a deliberate dig.

"Thank you," Audrey said in her kindest voice, as if the nurse had been as sweet as sugar. When she turned, however, the smile faded away. Some people really struggled with that innocent-until-proven-guilty concept.

She felt as if she were walking through wet cement as she headed for her mother's room. On the drive to Nashville then the flight to Denver, she'd played endless possible conversations in her mind and still didn't know what would be the first words out of her mouth.

When she reached Room 514, she met another nurse coming out of the room with a blood-pressure cuff and thermometer. A uniformed guard followed her. The sight of the guard there, as if he were protecting the nurse from her mother, hit Audrey like a large fist to the chest. Yes, her mother was a criminal, but she wasn't a violent woman. It wasn't as if she was going to strangle a nurse with oxygen tubing.

"Are you here to see Mrs. York?" the pixyish blond nurse asked Audrey.

She almost denied it and kept walking down the hall, but then she chided herself for being such an enormous chicken. "Yes."

"I need to see your ID, please," the guard said.

Audrey pulled her wallet out and handed the man her driver's license. After examining it and his list, he handed it back.

"I have to check your bag."

Audrey wanted to ask him if she was going to be subjected to a cavity search, too, but she bit down on her lower lip and handed him her purse instead.

"You're her daughter, aren't you?" the nurse asked.

Audrey braced for more hostility, so she was unprepared for the genuine smile the young woman offered her.

"She's talked about you a lot when she's been awake, showed me your picture. You're even prettier in person."

"Uh…thank you."

Audrey glanced at the nurse's name tag. Holly—the name fit her outward appearance and personality.

The guard, satisfied that she wasn't packing a gun or a shank, handed her purse back to her and took his seat in the chair next to the door.

Holly placed her hand on Audrey's arm in a friendly gesture. "It's good that you've come. I can tell she's been wanting to talk to you."

Audrey didn't know how to feel about that. Did her mom want forgiveness? Could she give her mother that? Or was there too much hurt and betrayal still between them?

She glanced at the door that led into her mother's room. "How is she?"

"Tired. The chemotherapy has been a bit rough on her."

Audrey sucked in a sharp breath. "She's taking chemo?"

"Yes. She has a tough path ahead of her, but the cancer was caught in time if she responds well to the chemo."

Audrey met Holly's eyes. "When will you know if she's responding well?"

"Probably a couple more treatments. I'll let Dr. Sandefur know you have some questions for him. He's your mom's oncologist."

"Thank you."

With an encouraging pat on Audrey's arm, Holly made her way toward the nurses' station. Audrey wished she could tell her how much it had meant for her not to look at Audrey like a criminal. In fact, she hadn't even sounded accusatory when talking about her mom. Holly struck her as the type of nurse who looked at patients as people who needed her help, no matter who they were or what they'd done outside the hospital's walls.

Audrey stood in the corridor staring at the door for a long time before she took a deep, painful breath and walked in.

She'd known her mother was sick, but she still wasn't prepared for how small and old Thomasina looked lying in the bed, hooked up to monitors and IV poles. Tears popped into Audrey's eyes despite how estranged they'd become.

At first she thought her mother was asleep, but then her eyes opened. She squinted them as if she couldn't see, and Audrey wondered if the cancer or chemo treatments had somehow affected her mother's vision.

"Audrey?" Thomasina uttered the single word in a disbelieving voice.

"Yeah."

Tears pooled in Thomasina's eyes, the sight of that emotion sucker punching Audrey so hard she found it difficult to breathe.

"How did you know?"

"A reporter showed up on my doorstep."

Thomasina closed her eyes. "I'm sorry."

Audrey didn't ask why her mother hadn't let her know herself. She'd told her mother she never wanted to talk to her again. Those spiteful words still echoed in Audrey's memory. She took a few more steps into the room and tossed her purse on the floor as she seated herself in a recliner in the corner.

She had no idea where to start, if she could even have a conversation with her mother without her blood pressure shooting through the roof. And no matter what her mother had done, it was just wrong to have it out with someone as sick as her.

Thomasina opened her eyes again and shifted so she could raise the head of the bed. The pain on her face as she moved caused an ache of guilt to surge through Audrey, as well. When her mother settled back against her pillow, she let out a slow breath and offered a small smile, one Audrey felt sure was forced.

"I'm glad you came. I'm surprised."

Audrey looked down at her hands clasped in her lap. "I didn't know if I would, not at first."

Thomasina gripped the edge of her blanket. "I

wouldn't have blamed you if you'd stayed away, after everything you went through because of me. I was afraid I wouldn't be able to tell you how sorry I am."

"You said that before." Audrey tried to ignore the fact that now there was a ring of truth to her mother's words. A year ago, they'd seemed to be uttered because that's what was expected.

"Yes, I did. I might have meant it then, too, on a superficial level." She sounded ashamed and breathless.

Audrey wondered if the latter was a result of her illness. She looked her mother in the eye. "And now?"

"Hurting you is the great regret of my life. Not a day goes by when I don't wish I could turn back the clock and undo everything, not fall into the trap that I did."

"Trap?"

"I…" Her mom winced with what must have been another pain in her chest. "I've been meeting with a therapist since I was sentenced."

Audrey got to her feet and paced across the room, her shoes still squeaking. "I'm not sure I can handle hearing about how something in your childhood made you steal money from thousands of people."

They were quiet for several seconds until Thomasina responded. "I deserved that." She took a shaky breath that made her sound like the sick woman she was. "I have no right to ask, but I would like to request one favor."

"And that is?"

"I've been thinking about what I wanted to say to you if I ever saw you again for a long time. All I ask is that you let me say those things. If you want to leave afterward, I will respect that and never bother you or expect you to visit me again." The words came out in a rush, as if she was afraid Audrey would interrupt and rob her of the opportunity to speak. Sadness hid behind the strong front Thomasina was presenting.

Audrey rubbed her bare, damp arms against the coolness of the room. Without saying anything, she walked back to the chair and sat. She'd listen. After all, she'd traveled a long way.

Thomasina sighed and clasped her hands together. "If I could go back, I would have done things so differently. I think I would have stayed at that secretarial job and just volunteered at the church like most normal, church-going folks do. If I'd known how growing the ministry would have clouded my judgment, I would have never headed down that path."

Flashes of battered women hugging their children at shelters, of health-education centers in AIDS-riddled Africa and little girls in developing countries attending school for the first time played through Audrey's mind.

"But you helped lots of people." The words tumbled out of her mouth, the need to defend at least part of her mother's past surfacing.

"I hurt a lot, too, made people doubt supporting worthwhile programs." She looked up at Audrey with deep sorrow in her eyes. "And I hurt the person who means the most to me. If I had to live in a cardboard box in an alley in order to have never hurt you, I'd do it gladly."

"Why did you do it, Mom?" Audrey had asked this

question before, but her mother had been in avoidance mode in those days after her arrest and had never given a satisfactory answer.

Thomasina exhaled a slow breath. "I believed I deserved it. At least that's what I thought at the time. I know now that I was weak and let myself be influenced by what those around me were telling me. They said that I'd helped so many people that I deserved to live life a little easier."

Audrey pictured the large mountaintop home, the rock-and-timber construction, the huge picture windows affording gorgeous views, the sumptuous leather sofas and giant fireplaces. "A little easier doesn't equal posh."

Her mother lowered her head, like a scolded child. "I know. It's just…you lose all perspective once you start down that road. I should have never pulled myself out of the field. Maybe if I'd kept doing the hands-on work instead of staying in the office, I wouldn't have given in to temptation. I would have been happier."

Something about that admission caused an incredible sadness to well within Audrey. "So all the things didn't make you happy?"

"No. Theresa—she's my therapist—she helped me realize the deeper reason behind my surrounding myself with wealth and lots of beautiful things. Despite being around people all the time, I was lonely. I was trying to fill a void that your dad's death left in my life, and there was nothing that could do that." Thomasina shook her head and sniffled. "In a million years, I wouldn't have figured out that's what I was doing. But when she suggested that as the reason, it clicked into place like the last piece of a jigsaw puzzle I'd been trying to finish for more than twenty years."

Thomasina twisted the edge of her covers. "I was so ashamed," she whispered, her voice raw with emotion. "I knew your father would be so disappointed in what I'd done, what I'd become. How I'd hurt you, his little girl."

Audrey hadn't expected a discussion of their estrangement to come up quite so soon, but she was glad they were diving right in. Tiptoeing around it would only make her stomach churn and the anxiety build until it was difficult to breathe.

"I believed in you, in what you were doing," Audrey said, not cloaking the hurt coloring her words. "When I found out the charges against you were true, I'd never felt so betrayed in my life."

"I know, and I'm sorry that I didn't have this conversation with you then. I…" Thomasina shook her head. "I felt like I wasn't even in my body before, like all of these things were going on around me and I was watching them from a distance. I know it doesn't make sense, but I felt as if I hadn't actually been me in a long, long time."

"What about now?"

Thomasina laid her head back against her pillow. "I'm more at peace, especially since I've talked to you. I don't expect people's forgiveness. I know it's hard to forgive another person when that person has betrayed your trust. I have no problem with serving my sentence or with dying first if that's my fate."

Fear gripped Audrey at the thought of her mother's death. "Don't talk like that."

"Death is nothing to fear, not when you've made things right." Thomasina sounded like she had in the early days of her ministry, tender and reassuring. "And that's what I'm trying to do. I've arranged for what's left of the estate and all my holdings to be sold and the money to go back to the people it came from. I'm sorry, but there will be nothing left for you."

Audrey sat back and crossed her arms. "I don't want money."

"I know, dear, but it's a sad thing that I messed up so much that I have nothing to pass on to my only child."

Audrey took a deep breath, released it slowly as she looked out the window toward a cloudless blue sky that had appeared in the wake of the rainstorm. "You have given me something." She paused, marveling at what she was about to say. "Honesty."

"You believe me, then?"

She looked back at her mother. "Yes. I'm not saying all the hurt is magically gone. I lost a lot because of what happened. But I'm tired, Mom. Tired of being angry, tired of always looking over my shoulder like the past is going to sneak up on me. Just plain tired."

The door to the room opened, and Holly walked in followed by the guard. The clock on the wall revealed an hour had already passed.

"Time for your vitals," Holly said in a chirpy voice that reminded Audrey for some reason of a bright yellow finch.

The guard stood in the corner and watched as Holly

checked Thomasina's blood pressure and temperature, then all the various tubes and IV bags.

"Well, looking good." Holly squeezed Thomasina's hand. "You need to get some rest soon, you hear. I know you're anxious to catch up with your daughter, but I bet she won't mind if you snatch a few winks." Holly glanced at Audrey with meaning in her eyes.

Thomasina seemed on the verge of arguing. But when her mom shifted, Audrey noticed how pale and drawn her mother's face was. Like the past hour had drained her of what little color she had to begin with.

Audrey stood. "I'll go grab a bite, make a couple of phone calls. Be back in a little while. We'll talk more then."

Her mother's eyes were drifting closed even as she nodded.

The guard followed them out of the room. Audrey faced him as he shut the door behind them.

"Do you think she's going to get up and make a run for it?" Defending her mother after all this time felt strange, like stretching a muscle that had been allowed to atrophy.

"It's policy, ma'am." He didn't say it in an ugly way, just matter-of-fact.

Audrey could understand that for murderers, gang members, people who posed a genuine flight risk. None of those things applied to her mother, but she said nothing further and fell into step alongside Holly.

"Would you like some coffee?"

Audrey shook her head, almost too tired to do so. "I don't drink coffee. I think I'll go for a walk."

"She'll probably be awake again in an hour or two. It's critical that she get plenty of rest now."

Audrey nodded. "I understand."

Once outside the hospital, though, she didn't know which way to go. Kind of like her relationship with her mother. She'd imagined screaming out her feelings at her mom so many times, but when she'd faced her, it hadn't seemed worth what it would cost her mother. Her mom seemed truly apologetic. While Audrey was still hurt by everything that had happened, she found the anger slipping away. It had been a part of her for so long that she now felt like there were empty holes all through her.

*Holes you can fill with love.*

Brady's face came to her. She ached to feel his arms around her again, a pillar of strength and positive human contact. As she headed down the street, she wondered what he was doing right now. Was he with his dad or back in Kingsport taking care of necessary business? Was he thinking about her? Did she dare hope he was missing her as much as she was him?

After getting a chicken-salad sandwich from a shop a couple of blocks from the hospital, she crossed the street to a park and sat on a bench after wiping off the leftover raindrops with a napkin. As she chewed, she thought back to the dinner they'd missed together. Maybe they could have a romantic meal alone when she got back. She smiled at that and savored the anticipation.

Had she ever experienced this jittery, euphoric feeling when thinking of Darren? Now that she looked back, he fell more into the category of comfortable.

Yes, she'd loved him, but now she wondered if she'd been *in love* with him. What she'd felt for him at the height of their relationship paled in comparison to what she felt toward Brady here at the beginning of theirs.

She hurried through the rest of her sandwich then pulled her cell phone from her purse. A smile tugged at the edges of her mouth as she dialed Brady's number.

"Hello," he answered, sounding distracted.

Audrey pushed away the doubt demons that whispered to her. "Hey, it's me."

"Oh, hi," he said. It sounded as if he stopped walking. "How are you?"

"Okay." She was surprised when she realized that was true. Things weren't perfect by any means, but she was doing better than she'd anticipated while walking to the hospital that morning. "You?"

"Busy as heck, but that's a good thing."

"Did I catch you at a bad time?" *He's not avoiding me, he's not avoiding me.*

"No, it's fine." The sound of rustling in the background was followed by that of an opening and closing door. "How's your mom?" he asked with what sounded like heartfelt concern.

The image of her mother in her hospital bed dimmed Audrey's mood. "Tired, drained." She raised her hand and pressed against her forehead. "I haven't talked to a doctor yet, so I don't know any specifics other than she's doing some chemo treatments. The nurse did tell me they caught it in time if Mom responds well to the chemo."

"Have you had time to talk to your mom?"

"Some. It…hasn't gone as I expected."

"So you're feeling unprepared."

Audrey smiled a little. "Are you sure you're not a shrink?"

"Last time I checked."

Her smile faded as she watched the traffic passing by the park. "She's been very apologetic, but it's hard to turn off everything I've been feeling for the past year and go on like nothing happened."

"You don't have to. It's one of those one-day-at-a-time things."

"How'd you get so wise?"

"Good clean living."

Audrey laughed. "Thank you."

"For what?"

"Just being there. Letting me talk your ear off."

"Anytime." The way he said it made Audrey dream of forever, a forever with Brady. What would he think if he could read her thoughts? Would he run for the hills, or was it possible those types of thoughts had occurred to him, too?

"I miss you," she said. The words revealed so much of what she felt for him that it left her feeling exposed and vulnerable.

"I miss you, too."

Tears welled in Audrey's eyes because she wanted him next to her so badly, wanted to feel his arms around her, giving her strength to face the coming days.

But this was something she had to do on her own. This wasn't Brady's gauntlet to run.

BY THE TIME SHE WALKED around downtown Denver some more, thinking about her life, Brady and what her mother was facing, and returned to the hospital, half the afternoon was gone. After the guard searched her purse again—in case she'd gone out to buy a gun—she walked into her mom's room to see she was awake again and nibbling on some crackers.

"Did you sleep well?"

"Right up until I had to puke my guts up."

"The chemo?" Audrey heard the sympathy in her voice, which revealed she was at least on her way to forgiving her mom.

Thomasina nodded.

"What has the doctor said? I haven't seen him."

Her mom tossed a half-eaten cracker on the table situated across her legs. "It's stage three, but they think the chemo will work to get rid of anything the surgery didn't remove. At least there's a decent-percentage chance of that."

"You had surgery?" What else did she not know?

"Yeah, three days ago. Actually, I'm surprised I'm still here. I figure they'll transfer me to the prison infirmary as soon as Dr. Sandefur says it's okay."

Audrey sank into the recliner. "A prison doesn't seem like the best place for you to get well."

"Well, honey, I'm a convicted felon. That's how it works." Thomasina seemed so accepting of her fate, like she'd come to terms with it.

Audrey thought she had, too, long ago when her mother had been led from the courtroom after her sentence was handed down. But now she wasn't so sure. An older woman with cancer in prison seemed so cold and heartless.

"Don't look so upset, pumpkin," her mother said, using the childhood nickname Audrey hadn't heard in years. "I'm fine with it, really. I made mistakes, and I have to pay for them. And if it's my destiny to die from this disease, I will accept that."

"Don't, Mom." Her mom might be ready to accept that fatal destiny, but Audrey wasn't.

"It's a possibility we have to face. Ignoring it won't make it go away."

"Well, I don't want to face it unless absolutely necessary."

"Okay."

Silence settled on the room until Thomasina said, "So, tell me how you've been. I've wondered so many times where you were and what you were doing."

Audrey sat without speaking for several moments, again staring out the window. Did she want to open up about her new home, to bring her mother into that life?

She imagined Brady's voice, telling her that the past was in the past, that she could carve out her future on her own terms. Just because her mom knew about her new life didn't mean the ugliness of the old one would seep in and taint it.

"I moved to the mountains," she said.

"Oh, you always loved it up there."

Audrey didn't hold anything back. If she was going to share her story with her mother, that story was going to include the bad as well as the good. It was the only way she felt she could purge the negative feelings that still lingered toward her mom, the only way she could truly move forward and start rebuilding their relationship.

She divulged all the details about the weeks after her mom's trial—the inability to get a job, the loss of friends, the suspicion in everyone's eyes and the breakup with Darren. She was glad to get that part of the story out and move on to her new life in Willow Glen. To help her mother visualize the setting, she pulled out her digital camera and sat on the edge of the bed. As she scrolled through the pictures, she kept up a running commentary about the mill, Willow Glen, her plans for the café, even Nelson and Brady.

"This Brady, he's quite the hunk," her mom said as Audrey stopped on a photo of Brady posing with his dad, both of them covered in sweat and sawdust.

Audrey jerked her gaze to her mother. "Mom!"

"Well, he is. I've got eyes," she said in a playful way.

Audrey laughed. It felt odd and strangely wonderful to laugh with her mother again.

They talked about all the renovations the mill had undergone, Audrey's plans for the future, the upcoming opening.

"I'm sure it's going to be beautiful and very successful," Thomasina said. She sounded tired, like the conversation had drained her again.

Audrey touched her mother's arm. "You need to get some rest."

Thomasina started to argue, but Audrey squeezed

her mom's arm gently. "I'll stay here, don't worry. We'll talk more when you wake up."

Thomasina placed her hand atop Audrey's. "Thank you."

"For what?"

"For being here. I didn't expect you to visit, but I did long for it."

Overcome with a love she hadn't felt toward her mother in a long time, Audrey leaned forward and kissed her mom on the forehead. "Sleep now."

AUDREY SLEPT in small snatches. A hospital had to be the absolute worst place to get any decent rest. Except a prison, perhaps.

After leaving the room briefly to get some dinner in the hospital cafeteria, she returned to find her mom still sleeping. Not wanting to disturb her but not able to face the uncomfortable recliner again, she instead slid onto the wide windowsill. She watched as the last vestiges of daylight disappeared behind the Front Range and night descended.

If she got away from Denver's lights and traveled toward those mountains in the distance, she'd bet she could see a sky full of twinkling stars. The same canopy of stars that watched over Brady back in Tennessee.

Wanting to see his face, she pulled out her camera and scrolled through the photos until she came to the one of him and Nelson outside the mill. She smiled when she remembered their good-natured argument about who stank the most after that particular day of work. She ran her thumb over his picture as if she could feel the man behind the image.

"You care about him a lot, don't you?"

Audrey jumped. "You're awake." She sounded like a squeaky teenager caught sucking face on the darkened front porch.

"Yes, and it seems I've been asleep a long time."

"That's okay," Audrey said, recovering her normal tone of voice. "You need your rest."

Thomasina raised her hand and pointed at the camera in Audrey's hands. "If his picture can make you smile like that, I can only imagine how the real man does."

Audrey turned off the camera and dropped it into her purse. "How do you know I'm looking at Brady?" She wondered if she sounded as casual as she hoped.

"As much as you love your new place, I doubt it causes that goofy smile I just saw."

"I didn't have a goofy smile."

"Yes, you did. And that's a good thing. After what you've been through, you deserve a wonderful man to make you happy."

"I can make myself happy."

"To some extent. But trust me, there is nothing like the feeling of loving and being loved, truly loved, by a man." Thomasina twirled the modest wedding band she still wore two decades after she'd lost her husband. Even with all the money she'd had at her disposal, she'd never replaced it with something more expensive. Perhaps that fact said more about her mom than anything else. It warmed Audrey's heart to think about the love her parents had shared, but she still wondered about the loneliness her mother had endured after her husband's death.

She turned more toward her mom. "Why didn't you ever get married again?"

"Because I never found a man who could live up to your father. I still love him and think about him every day."

"I think he would have wanted you to be happy."

"He would have wanted you to be happy, too. Nice redirection of the conversation, by the way." Her mom shook her finger at Audrey, still able to read her without much effort.

Audrey turned her gaze out the window. "Yes, I like him, okay?"

"Does he feel the same?"

"He acts like it."

"Then what's the problem?"

It felt weird to talk to her mom about Brady. She hadn't had another woman to talk to in a long time, so despite the weirdness it also came as a relief.

"We haven't known each other very long, so I don't know if what I'm feeling is real or if I'm grasping at…at the first person who hasn't looked at me like I might be a criminal."

"Does it feel real? Are you all giddy inside, like you want to dance all the time because you can't contain the joy?"

Audrey sighed, afraid to admit the truth. "Yes."

"But?"

"After Darren, it's hard to believe I won't turn around

to find Brady gone one day. And the thing is I couldn't blame him. He and his father are well respected in the community." She shook her head slowly. "Brady's working on a big project, a Christian retreat center. I don't want to endanger that or their reputations."

Her mother caught her gaze and gave her one of those looks that was one part love, one part mother knows best. "I know you've lost friends because of what happened, but not everyone is so fickle. And all men aren't like Darren."

"I know." She really did. Even if things didn't work out with Brady, she'd never put him in the same category as Darren. She couldn't imagine him being that cold and unfeeling in the wake of some very nice times together.

"It's more than a simple crush, isn't it? You love him."

"I don't know. I think so, but how can I be sure? How can it be possible when we haven't known each other very long?"

"I've never seen a manual that says two people have to know each other X amount of days or weeks or months before they can fall in love. It took me exactly one date to know your father was the man for me. Nothing had ever felt so right." Her voice sounded dreamy, like she was floating back through time to those long-ago days.

"You didn't think it was merely infatuation?"

Thomasina shook her head. "No. I'd felt that before, and this was different. Deeply different."

Audrey looked up at the sky and thought she could see some of the brighter stars beyond the city's lights.

"If you love him, tell him," her mom said. "Life is too short to hide love inside yourself. It should be shared."

Audrey thought about those words all night as she watched her mother sleep. Thomasina had lost the love of her life much too soon, and Audrey's heart ached at the idea of losing Brady before she even had a chance to really be with him. As dawn crept over the plains east of Denver, she decided to tell Brady everything when she got home. And hope that he felt as much for her as she did for him.

When her mom woke again, Audrey went to sit beside her on the bed. "I thought about what you said, and I'm going to tell him when I get home. I want to do it in person."

Thomasina lifted her hand to Audrey's cheek. "I'm glad."

Audrey leaned over and hugged her mom. "I'm going to the hotel to get a shower, but I'll be back later."

Thoughts about her mom's health and her plans to tell Brady that she was falling in love with him had her so occupied when she stepped outside the hospital's doors that she didn't notice the reporters until it was too late.

"Miss York, how ill is your mother?"

"Are you here to reconcile with her?"

"Are you the person investigators are taking a closer look at?"

Audrey threw up her hand to block the camera shots and hurried toward the street crossing. Anger surged through her. Someone had told the press that she was here. Horrible memories of being hounded in the aftermath of her mom's arrest hit her and propelled her faster toward her hotel.

But the sidewalk leading to her hotel was blocked by more reporters. Panic pressed in from all sides. Not knowing where she was headed, she turned left and ran away from the questions and cameras. She turned corner after corner, likely getting herself more and more lost. She didn't even turn to see if anyone was following her. It didn't matter. Once she was running, she couldn't seem to stop. Not until the wheezing began in her lungs.

She slowed then stopped, grabbed the top of a wrought-iron fence while she concentrated on slowing her breathing, calming herself so she didn't have to resort to the inhaler in her purse. As she'd suspected, no one had pursued her this far, but she still couldn't face going back. Not yet. But where was she supposed to go? Just wander the unfamiliar streets of downtown Denver?

She lifted her head and noticed she'd stopped in front of an old stone church. The sign said St. Elizabeth's. She wasn't Catholic, but it didn't matter. She found herself heading toward the doors of what was likely the last place anyone would look for her. The air was immediately cooler when she stepped inside. She walked softer as she covered the length of the center aisle then slid into the front pew. Within the old walls, the world outside fell away.

But not her hurt, not her questions about why the reporters felt the need to hound her, why her mother was sick, why something always happened to ruin her happiness. She wasn't even angry anymore. She was just tired and confused. It took tremendous effort to lift her head and look at the sunlight streaming in the window.

"Why?" she whispered.

# Chapter Ten

Brady dropped onto the couch, too exhausted to even open the fast-food bag containing his greasy dinner. What he wouldn't give for some of Audrey's delicious cooking right now. Since she'd been gone, his long hours had him subsisting on coffee and junk food of every variety.

But he wanted to be caught up with his work, maybe even be a bit ahead of the game, when Audrey returned so he could spend time with her. That was if she still wanted to after being away.

He flicked on the TV as the national news was beginning. Conflict, negative economic numbers, blah, blah, blah. Same news, different day. He was about to flip the channel when the photo that flashed on the screen behind the news anchor stopped him cold. He turned up the volume.

"Family reconciliation or a move to cover her trail? That's the question many are asking tonight after

Audrey York, estranged daughter of former TV evangelist Thomasina York, was spotted leaving the Denver hospital where the elder York is undergoing treatment for breast cancer."

The rest of the words making up the report faded away as Brady focused on the footage of Audrey, her startled expression as she'd emerged from the hospital to find cameras and microphones waiting for her. Her fleeing across the street, nearly being run over by traffic, to get away from the reporters.

Brady's fists clenched. Hadn't she been through enough?

He clicked off the TV and grabbed his phone. But she didn't answer either her cell or her hotel-room line. He sprang from the couch and paced his apartment, feeling absolutely useless and like he wanted to wring someone's neck, preferably the neck of one of those reporters.

When he placed another call, it was to Craig.

"What's up?"

"I've got to make a quick trip out of town. I'll be back in a couple of days."

"Whoa!" Craig said before Brady could hang up. "We've got the Lakeview ground-breaking in the morning, in case you forgot."

"I didn't. Sorry to bail, but this is more important."

"Audrey?"

"Yeah." He glanced at his watch as he ended the call before Craig could ask more questions. He had to pack and hit the road.

"I'M SO SORRY, honey," Thomasina said from the other end of the phone line. "I never thought about reporters. Why would they show up now? My case is old news."

"It's the new angle of investigators possibly arresting someone else. They think it might be me." Audrey tried to keep herself from sounding so drained, but she didn't fully succeed.

"That's ridiculous."

"In the absence of any other information…"

"They should be finished with this already." Thomasina sounded so agitated that Audrey worried about her. But something in what she'd said clicked.

"You know who it is?"

"Yes, but I had to keep quiet until they had the evidence to make an arrest."

All the possibilities ran through her head again, but she couldn't pinpoint one over another. How could she when she hadn't even suspected her mother? "Who is it?"

Her mother remained silent on the other end of the line.

"Mom?"

"Okay. It's Adam."

Audrey let out a slow, sad breath. Adam Quinn had been her mother's assistant for years, choosing to stay with her even when he got better job offers. She'd always thought it was devotion to her mom and the cause, but it now appeared otherwise. Was anyone what they seemed on the surface?

"They found more irregularities than what they could connect to me. Evidently he was skimming long before I started down my own wrong path."

"I'm so sorry, Mom." Adam had been like a son to Thomasina, even there by her side in the days after her mother's arrest when Audrey herself had pulled away.

"This in no way lessens how much I hurt you or my own mistakes, but I do know how that betrayal feels."

A knock on Audrey's door made her jump and stare at it as if the dead bolt would unlock itself and let in whoever had found her. "Listen, I've got to go. I'll call you later, and I'll come back to visit when I find another way in where I won't be seen."

Another knock, more insistent this time.

"No, you stay there until you hear from me." Thomasina sounded surprisingly forceful. "I'm going to see if they can get a move on with Adam's arrest. I don't want you to go through this anymore."

"Audrey?" said a male voice from the hallway.

Her gaze shot to the door. Had she finally cracked? Because that had sounded like Brady.

"Okay," she said to her mom and hung up.

"Audrey, are you in there?"

Her shaky legs carried her toward the door. When she reached it, she was afraid to look through the peephole, afraid that if she saw no one she'd know her mind had finally flown the coop.

With breath held, she leaned forward and peered through the peephole.

Brady stood on the other side of the door with a worried expression tightening his handsome face. Afraid he'd disappear if she didn't get the door open quickly, she fumbled with the lock before managing to fling the door wide.

"Brady?" she choked out, hardly able to believe her eyes.

He took her in his arms. "I'm here. Shh, it's okay." He guided her farther into the room and locked the door behind them. Then he pulled back and framed her face in his hands. "Are you all right?"

She nodded and blinked against happy tears. "I am now."

"I was worried about you. When I saw you on the news, you looked so scared."

The mention of the news shattered the wonderful spell of him showing up on her doorstep like a knight in shining armor. She broke contact and walked across the room, hating how reality catapulted fantasy out of the room.

"You shouldn't have come."

Brady took a few steps into the room. "Why? I thought you were glad to see me."

Audrey hugged herself. "I am, I really am. And that's why you should have stayed away."

He came up behind her and spun her to face him. Confusion pulled at his angular features. "You're not making any sense."

She closed her eyes and tried to find the right words. When she opened her eyes again, she looked up into his beautiful green ones. "I care about you a lot. That's why I don't want your life to be touched by all this mess."

"I'm a big boy, Audrey. I can take care of myself."

"But what if being associated with me hurts your business?"

"It won't."

"You don't know that."

He stared down at her, and her heart hurt so much to see that he realized she was right. With a touch so gentle it was hard to believe it belonged to a man like him, he caressed the curve of her jaw.

"Maybe not. But if that happens, we'll deal with it. I won't be bullied, and I won't let them bother you, either."

Audrey knew she should convince him to stay away for his own good, but she had no more strength left to try. She wanted him here, holding her, so she didn't have to face everything alone. She walked into his arms, and it felt like home.

"I STILL CAN'T BELIEVE you're here," Audrey said hours later as they lay on the bed together. They were still fully clothed and had done nothing more intimate than kiss, but that was what she needed.

"You've said that." He planted another gentle kiss on her lips. "About a dozen times."

"Well, I can't." She shifted so she could meet his eyes. "I keep thinking I'm going to wake up and it'll have all been a dream."

"So I'm the stuff of dreams, huh?" He winked at her, reminding her of the way he'd teased the day they'd gone canoeing.

She gave him a wicked look. "I'm not telling."

"I have ways of making you talk." He rolled so that he was leaning over her.

She giggled and swatted at him, to little effect. He kissed her, ending her mock struggle.

When Brady pulled away, he stared down at her, a hint of seriousness filling his eyes.

"What?"

"I need to apologize to you."

"If this is about missing dinner again, you've already apologized."

"It is, but it's more than that." Brady rolled onto his back and stared at the ceiling.

Nervousness surged through her as she lifted onto one elbow to look at him. "What is it?"

He took a deep breath, then let it out. "I deliberately stayed away from dinner."

"Oh?" Audrey tried to ignore the punch to the gut and the ache that invaded her heart.

"Doubt got the better of me." With another exhaled breath, Brady continued. "I was engaged once, in love, the whole thing. But a few days before the wedding, I caught my fiancée kissing another guy when she thought I wasn't around. I was about to confront them when what they said made it worse. Seems the plan was for Ginny to marry me, get her hands on my money, drain me dry, then leave with the other guy."

"That's horrible." How could any woman do that to Brady? Hadn't this Ginny grasped what she had in him?

He closed his eyes for a moment before meeting

hers. "I saw her that night. Hadn't seen her in probably a couple of years. I let it mess with my head. Hell, thought it was some sort of sign that I was messing up again."

Audrey swallowed against the dryness in her throat. "What changed your mind?"

"Partly what I already knew deep down. Partly Craig telling me I was an idiot and he was going after you if I didn't."

Despite the seriousness of the conversation, a laugh escaped Audrey before she could cover her mouth. "Sorry," she said against her palm when Brady looked at her.

It took a moment, but he smiled. "No way was I letting him make that move. I'd hate to have to punch my best friend."

Audrey lowered her hand. "Defending my honor?" she asked playfully. "How chivalrous of you."

Brady rolled toward her, sending her onto her back. "Had nothing to do with chivalry." He stared into her eyes, making her heart flutter with the intensity. "I really am sorry."

She lifted her hand to his cheek. "I think Ginny was the idiot, not you."

He lowered his lips to hers, and gradually the kiss grew more heated. It felt so good, so right. Oh, how she loved this man.

Someone knocked on the door, and Audrey stiffened.

"Ignore it. They'll go away."

But the person knocked again. And it wasn't hotel

staff, because Audrey had placed the Do Not Disturb sign on the door handle even before Brady had arrived.

"Just let me peek out the peephole."

Brady rolled over and off the bed. He followed Audrey as she headed for the door as quietly as she could. When she looked out this time, she saw the top of a blond head. She motioned to Brady it was okay and unlocked the door.

"Holly, what are you doing here?" she asked with her heart beating hard. Had something happened to her mom?

"I'm your chauffeur," the little nurse said.

"Huh?"

"I heard about what happened, and I offered to drive you over to the back entrance of the hospital. There's only a couple of reporters left, and they're in the front of the building." Audrey sensed movement behind her, and then Holly's eyes widened. "Whoa! Your mom was right. He is a hottie."

Audrey's face flushed, and she imagined Brady shifting uncomfortably behind her.

"That's nice of you to offer," Audrey said, trying to direct the conversation back to the rear-door drop-off. "But why?"

Holly made a flippy motion with her hand. "Oh, you know, because saving lives on a daily basis isn't enough excitement for me."

Audrey smiled. "Well, I wouldn't want to deprive you of a little excitement. Come on in. I'll be ready in a moment."

"You know, I think I'll wait in the garage. Space

C12." She made a casual gesture toward her hair and winked before turning around and leaving.

What the...? Audrey reached up and realized her hair was messed up from lying on the bed. Brady snickered behind her. She turned and swatted him on the arm. "You let me go to the door like that?"

He smiled wider and reached around her to shut the door. As it clicked closed, he grabbed her in his arms and laid a kiss on her that had her wondering if she could postpone the trip back to the hospital.

Though it pained her to do so, she pulled away. "I've got to go."

"Want me to go with you?"

Audrey stopped her progress toward the bathroom. "Do you want to?"

"It's totally up to you. I could come in handy." He flexed his biceps.

She laughed. "While the thought of you tossing reporters left and right like a superhero is, admittedly, a nice one, I think we need to fly under the radar."

He closed the distance between them and took her hands in his. "I don't want you to have to face everything alone."

The crazy question—did he mean for only today or forever?—ran through her head.

"Plus," he continued, "I've got to meet the woman who thinks I'm a hottie."

Audrey pushed against his chest then walked into the bathroom and closed the door in his face. But she smiled at his laughter on the other side of the door.

BRADY FOCUSED on the warmth of Audrey's hand in his as they followed Holly through a succession of hospital corridors to the fifth floor. When they reached the hallway where Thomasina York's room was located, Holly turned and gave them a bright smile.

"Mission accomplished," she said.

"Thank you," Audrey said as she gave Holly a hug.

"No problem. I think I missed my calling as a secret agent."

Audrey shook her head. "No. I think you're right where you should be."

Holly squeezed Audrey's hands. "So are you." She met his glance, too, as if the words were for him, as well. He felt she was right, but how could she know that when she'd just met him?

Unless Audrey had been talking about him. Well, she evidently had if her mother knew what he looked like. His curiosity flared. He'd have to ask her later— when they were alone.

After Holly left, they walked farther down the hall. The guard stationed outside made it obvious which room was Thomasina York's. A guard for a woman with cancer seemed excessive.

"He's there as much to keep people out as to keep her in," Audrey said.

"Reading my mind?"

"I wondered the same thing when I saw him. It made me mad." Audrey stopped in the middle of the hall.

"What's wrong?"

"I didn't think about the list. You won't be able

to go into Mom's room. Only certain people are allowed."

"It's okay. I can wait for you."

She shook her head. "I don't know how long I'll be. You should go back to the hotel." He thought he detected some nervousness in her expression when she looked up at him. "Or maybe you should go home."

Was she sending him away? Did she not want him here?

He cupped her chin. "Take however long you need. Don't worry about me."

A close-lipped smile tugged at her lips, and he wished he could do something to make her life easier, so that she could smile wide and be happy every day.

"I think I've developed a guilt complex over the past year," she said. "I keep thinking about how you don't deserve having to deal with the craziness of my life, how you're spending so much time away from your home, your business. I know they mean a lot to you."

"There are other things that mean a lot to me, too." He wanted to show her how much, but they were in the middle of a busy hospital. So he hoped the tender kiss on her forehead would give her some idea. "I'll go back to the hotel, even do some work by phone if it'll make you feel less guilty."

She laughed a little, the warmth of her breath seeping through his shirt. "Yes, it would."

"Call me if you need me."

She nodded then walked the rest of the way to her mother's room.

He turned to leave, planning to make good use of the hotel's business center until Audrey returned.

"Wait!"

He looked back to see Audrey holding up her index finger. "I have an idea." She tossed her purse at the guard and darted into her mother's room.

What was she doing?

He'd started walking toward the room again when she exited, excitement brightening her eyes. "Come on."

"Ma'am, he's not on the list," the guard said.

"He doesn't have to be to stand in the hall, does he?" Audrey took a few steps, grabbed Brady's hand and pulled him to the open doorway. "Mom, this is Brady."

An older woman with short silver hair who lay attached to an assortment of tubes and monitors raised her hand. "Hello. So you're the young man who has been helping my Audrey with her new project?"

He wondered why she'd phrased the end of the question the way she had. Then he realized she was being careful that the guard or anyone passing by didn't learn any of the details of where Audrey now lived. She was giving her daughter a chance for that new life and some privacy. Despite what she'd done in the past, he immediately liked Thomasina York.

"Yes, ma'am. My father and I."

"Sounds like he raised a fine son."

They talked like that for a few minutes until Brady noticed passersby beginning to stare and peek into the room, curious about the occupant being guarded by a law enforcement officer.

"I think it's time I left," he said, low so that his voice wouldn't carry down the corridor.

He could see the argument forming in Audrey's mind, but nodded to the side to indicate a curious couple walking by.

"Oh, okay. I'll see you later?" The way she phrased her words as a question nearly broke his heart, as if he would suddenly realize this had all been a mistake and flee back to Tennessee without telling her. He could kick himself for even having made her doubt him.

"Definitely." This time, he didn't care who saw them, her mom included. He leaned down and kissed her on the lips. Not how he really wanted to, but more than a peck.

Someone whistled. They broke the kiss and looked over to see Holly walking down the hall with a "Who, me? I didn't do anything" look on her face.

To avoid more comments from the peanut gallery, he dropped a quick kiss on Audrey's hand. She smiled at him when he released her. That smile would follow him all the way back to the hotel.

AUDREY WATCHED Brady walk down the hall, well aware that the guard and her mother were watching her. She didn't care. Despite all that her mother was facing and the lingering snatches of hurt from the past year, she felt as light as air.

She and the guard didn't make eye contact when he handed her purse back as she reentered her mother's room. After she shut the door, she noticed her mother grinning.

"If I were to venture a guess, I'd say that boy does like

you," Thomasina said, sounding much as she had when she'd teased Audrey about boys during high school.

Audrey couldn't erase the smile taking over her face. But, then, she didn't try too hard, either. She didn't even mind her mother's teasing. Thomasina looked a little better today, like the chemo drugs were doing their job and kicking the cancer out of her body like a bouncer at a bar.

Halfway through the morning, Carl Burton, her mother's attorney, arrived.

"I need to talk to you," he said to Thomasina without giving Audrey more than a glance.

"If this is what I think it's about, you can say it in front of Audrey."

He hesitated. "You told her?"

Thomasina sat up straighter. "She's my daughter. She's not going to repeat it to anyone."

"Last time I checked, you two weren't on the best of terms," Carl said, unfazed by Thomasina's mama-bear tone.

Audrey bristled, but forced herself to stay calm. After all, the man was right. His job was to work for his client's best interests, and the last time Audrey had seen him she hadn't been too concerned about her mother's welfare.

"Things change, Carl. Audrey has found it in her heart to work on our relationship. You can trust her."

"Fine." He shoved his hands into the pockets of his crisp suit pants. "The police are on their way to arrest Adam right now. They have enough to put him away for a long time."

Sadness pulled at Thomasina's face as she lowered

her eyes to the blanket covering her legs. "Then everything will be put to right."

Audrey wrapped her mother's hand between hers. She tried to remember when her mom would be up for parole. Would the parole board see her mother's remorse and how she was trying to make amends for what she'd done? Audrey decided she'd do whatever she could to make sure they granted her mother the ability to breathe free air again. Yes, she'd made a mistake, a big one, but she was genuinely sorry and didn't deserve to die behind prison walls.

Not that her mother would be dying anytime soon. Audrey couldn't face that possibility, so she flatly refused to believe the cancer would win. It wouldn't. She knew that.

"There's something else," Carl said.

Her mother looked up and understanding crept into her eyes. "They're sending me back."

"Yes, this afternoon." At this revelation, Carl's tone finally softened.

"Back?" Audrey's heart stuttered.

"To the prison infirmary," the attorney said. "They can manage her care there now."

It was one thing to see her mother in a hospital and used as a pincushion, but Audrey didn't know if she was strong enough to see her behind prison walls. Would she even be able to visit her mom while she was in the infirmary?

"It's too soon." As the words fell out of Audrey's mouth, she realized exactly how much she'd missed having her mother in her life the past year and how much it was going to hurt to not be able to see her every day.

Thomasina looked at Carl, and he got the message and left.

"It's okay," her mother said, trying to soothe. "We knew this would happen."

Audrey sprang to her feet and walked to the window. "I don't want to leave you out here all alone."

"I won't be alone, dear."

She stared back at her mom. "I don't think prison inmates and guards count."

"Sweetie, you have your own life to live."

"But…maybe I can sell the mill, find a place here. I could get a job doing…something."

"No."

Audrey crossed her arms and turned more fully toward her mother. "Why not?"

"Because a year of your life was already ruined because of me. I won't have you waste another minute." Thomasina shook her head. "If you could only see your face when you talk about your café, about those green mountains, the sound of the creek."

"It's beautiful here, too." She pointed out the window. "See, mountains."

"Yes, but no Brady."

The pain that stabbed her heart took Audrey by surprise. She didn't want to live without Brady, but how could she walk away from her mother when she had no one? When she was battling for her life?

Audrey let her mom believe she'd abandoned the

argument, but as she spent the rest of the morning with her she couldn't stop the tug-of-war going on inside herself. When the nurses and prison employees arrived to start her mom's transfer, she couldn't watch. She leaned over to hug her mom, fighting tears. Her mom did feel stronger than when Audrey had first arrived, so that was at least a positive sign. She wondered if her visit had helped give her mom the will to fight.

"I'll see you soon," Audrey said, her voice faltering.

Thomasina smoothed Audrey's hair. "You remember what I said. You grab your own happiness and don't let go. I love you, honey, and so does that young man."

"I love you, too, Mom." Before she broke down, Audrey fled the room and hurried down the hall, then another.

When she found an empty waiting room, she ducked into it and shut the door. She sat for several minutes staring at the wall in front of her without seeing it. She had no idea how much time passed before she came to a decision. Her hand shook as she dialed her cell phone.

BRADY PUT IN several hours at the hotel's business center, surprised how much he was able to accomplish while simultaneously thinking about Audrey. She'd trusted him enough to introduce him to her mom. That was a good sign, right?

On his way back to her room, he stopped by the hotel gift shop and bought a bouquet of flowers. They weren't expensive roses, but the colors of the mixed blooms reminded him of Audrey and her love of wildflowers.

His cell rang as he was placing the flowers on the room's desk. He glanced at the number and smiled.

"Hey. Miss me already?"

She laughed, but it was a faint laugh that let him know something was wrong. Had her mom taken a turn for the worse? She'd seemed okay a few hours ago.

"What is it?"

"I'm fine. They're just taking Mom back."

Back? "To the prison?"

"Yeah." She sniffled.

"When?"

"Right now. Actually, they may already be gone. I couldn't stay and watch."

"Where are you?"

"In a waiting room. I've been sitting here thinking for a while."

"Tell me where, and I'll be there as fast as I can."

"No, really. Holly is going to give me a ride to the prison. Her sister works there, in the infirmary."

He heard her take a shaky breath and worried about her asthma. "Are you okay?"

"I'll be fine. Really. It just all kind of surprised me."

"Is your mom ready to go back there?"

"Everyone says she is, which is good in a strange way."

"Because it means she's getting better."

"Yeah."

Brady sank onto the side of the bed. He sensed she

was trying to say something and having a difficult time. "You're going to stay here for a while longer."

"Yes. Before I can really move on, I need to know she's okay, that she's getting the best care she can considering the situation."

He understood, he really did. It didn't make him feel any better about leaving. Because that's what he knew she wanted to say—that it was time for him to go home. He had a life and work to get back to, and he couldn't put those on hold indefinitely.

"You know you can call me, right? Anytime, day or night."

"I know. And thank you."

She was just down the street, but he already missed her. He'd miss her until she returned to Willow Glen. To him.

## Chapter Eleven

Brady stopped hammering long enough to wipe the sweat from his forehead before it ran into his eyes. The ensuing quiet also allowed him to hear a vehicle coming down the lane toward the mill. The visitor proved to be his dad, probably here to deliver Audrey's mail from her mailbox. Brady slid another piece of lumber into place and started hammering again.

The gazebo was a surprise for Audrey when she returned home. He'd talked to her several times in the two weeks since he'd gotten back to Tennessee. While she always sounded spent, there was a sense of satisfaction in her voice, too. She and her mother were continuing to mend their relationship, and Audrey was doing all she could to make sure the powers that be took good care of her mom. She also was spreading the word that her mother was a changed woman, a good person at the core.

When he stopped hammering again, he noticed his dad wandering up to stand under the shade of the trees.

"That's coming along real nice," Nelson said.

"Yeah. Still a lot to do though." He was spending all his free moments working like mad to complete the gazebo before Audrey came home. And considering he didn't know when that might be, he was pushing himself to exhaustion.

"Any word on when Audrey's due back?"

"No."

"Interesting."

Brady knew that tone of voice. When he looked at his dad, yep, there was the smug look. His dad healed a bit more every day. More and more of his former personality resurfaced as a result. Brady wasn't so sure he was happy to see this aspect. He suspected he'd regret it, but he couldn't help asking, "What's interesting?"

"That even though there's no indication Audrey is coming back soon, you're working like a maniac to finish this gazebo."

"I just want to finish it so everything here will be done."

"I didn't know Audrey asked for help with the gazebo."

"She didn't."

"Mmm-hmm."

"Listen, she's dealing with a lot. When she gets back here, she'll be preparing to open the café. I don't think she'll have time to be out here building a gazebo by herself."

"Yes, but I got the impression this was a down-the-road project."

Brady let out an exasperated breath. "So what if it was? It's part of her overall dream for the place, so why not have it ready from the beginning?"

Nelson stuffed his hands into his pants pockets. "You know what I think?"

"I'm sure you're going to tell me."

"That this place and this woman have become your dream, too."

Brady stared at the half-finished roof of the gazebo, unable to deny it. He didn't want to. Sometime between that day he'd driven to the mill thinking the new woman in town was on the prowl for his recently widowed father and now, he'd fallen in love with her. And his entire attitude about commitment and risking eventual hurt had changed. What was that famous saying? It was better to have loved and lost than never to have loved at all.

Instead of rubbing it in or uttering an "I told you so," Nelson picked up the saw and consulted the plans for the gazebo.

"I hear having an extra set of hands makes work go a lot faster," he said.

As Brady watched his dad use a pencil to mark the cutting point on the board, he realized how much he owed the older man. After all, no matter how much Brady had resisted commitment since Ginny, his father had been the best example. But maybe he hadn't gotten serious again because he hadn't met the right woman.

Now he had. And as soon as he saw Audrey again, he was going to tell her.

AUDREY TURNED into the lane that led back to the mill, glad to almost be home. Exhaustion had her fantasizing about falling into her bed for hours of uninterrupted sleep. She'd been fighting to stay awake ever since she'd merged onto I-81 east of Knoxville. Now, the goal of blessed sleep was within two minutes of becoming reality.

The dark woods lining the lane welcomed her back, providing a comfort the bright city lights of Denver couldn't. Sure, the world wasn't perfect, but she'd made peace with both her mother and the situation. With Holly and her sister, Jessica, looking after Thomasina, Audrey was convinced her mother would receive good care. Her latest medical results were promising, showing that the chemotherapy was indeed doing its job.

And Audrey had met with both Carl and prison officials to make it known that her mother was truly remorseful and that she'd make sure the parole board knew that when the time came. Nobody could make promises, of course, but Audrey left those meetings hopeful.

Now that the other part of her life was on the right path, she had a lot to do here to prepare for the café's opening in two weeks. But not tonight. And maybe not tomorrow. She felt as if she'd been run through one of those old-timey wringer washing machines.

Her thoughts strayed to Brady, as they often did. She'd wondered how he was and if he'd still been working when she'd passed the Kingsport exits.

She'd called to let him know she was coming home tonight, but had to leave a message since he'd been on a work site. She'd done her best not to read anything into the fact that there had been no voice mails from him when she'd landed in Nashville—and no calls since, either. Trying not to give in to old insecurities, she'd resisted the urge to call him again. Maybe she'd pop by to see Nelson tomorrow and he'd mention that Brady had been working late or his cell phone had been run over by a bulldozer at a construction site.

She rubbed her eyes at the crazy notion. Wow, did she need some sleep. When she focused ahead of her as she pulled into the clearing, she wondered if her sleep-deprived state was making her see things, because Brady stood there waiting by his truck.

A surge of adrenaline pushed her fatigue out to arm's length. It was so good to see him.

She parked and got out of her car. "What brings you to my neck of the woods?"

"A little birdie told me you were coming home."

She leaned her hip against the car door. "And you decided to drive all the way up here instead of calling?"

"I was in the neighborhood," he said as he sauntered toward her.

She doubted that, but didn't argue the point. When he stepped close, she said, "It's good to see you."

He lifted a hand and caressed her cheek. "You, too. Though you look worn-out. Everything okay?"

"Yes, just tired. Long day."

She gave him the quick rundown of everything that had happened since she'd last talked to him—the latest on her mother's condition, how Adam's arrest and a statement by federal investigators had finally gotten the press off her tail and how she and her mother were going to handle the situation going forward.

"Sounds like the past isn't dogging your steps anymore," he said.

"No, it's finally put to rest." She yawned wide, making her jaw pop. "And speaking of rest…"

He traced his fingertip across her chin. "Do you think you could hold off sleep for a few more minutes?"

"Maybe. Depends on the reason." She gave him a saucy smile.

"Close your eyes."

She did as instructed, which made the sound of her beloved Willow Creek more pronounced. "You do know you're tempting fate here, right? If I close my eyes, I might fall asleep and you'll have to carry me to bed."

"I can think of worse things."

A delicious shiver raced up Audrey's spine. Brady took her hand and led her forward along the gravel drive. "What are you up to?"

"It's a surprise. Just keep your eyes closed."

"Okay." She tried to figure out what was going on based on the direction he was guiding her, and it felt like it wasn't toward the mill. What in the world?

"Stand here for a minute, and don't peek." Brady let go of her hand, and a couple of seconds later she heard a click. "Okay, open your eyes."

Her mouth fell open at the sight in front of her. Thousands of tiny white lights covered a finished white gazebo. White and pink tulle decorated the ceiling. She glanced down and saw the rock path leading from the driveway to the gazebo steps. Happy tears welled in her eyes.

"It's beautiful."

She walked forward feeling as if she'd dropped into some magical fairy world. She wouldn't have been surprised to see actual fairies flit by.

After walking the length of the stone path, she took the first step leading into the gazebo. "It's exactly how I pictured it." She shook her head slowly in disbelief. "How?"

"Dad helped, and Sophie did the poufy stuff," he said as he pointed toward the tulle.

She smiled. "Poufy stuff? That the technical term?"

"How would I know? If it's not sold at Lowe's or 84 Lumber, I'm clueless."

Audrey gazed at the gazebo some more, ran her hand along the freshly painted wood. "You three make a good team."

"So you like it?" Brady asked as he approached her.

She turned to find that her spot on the step had brought them eye to eye. "Like it? I love it."

"And I love you."

Audrey's breath got stuck trying to leave her lungs. "Oh, Brady." She leaned forward and kissed him with all the emotion flooding her body. In that moment, she realized how much she'd missed him while they'd been apart. And she had the strangest sensation that she'd missed him even before they'd met.

When the kiss ended, a small laugh escaped Brady, cooling her wet lips. "I take it by your response that you at least like me a little."

She leaned back and ran her fingertips along his strong jaw, soaked in every detail of this face that was never far from her mind. "I passed up liking you a little a long time ago."

"Yeah?" Brady teased.

"Yeah. In fact, I'm pretty sure I love you, too."

"Good, because I have something to ask you."

If she'd thought it was hard to breathe normally before, it was nothing in comparison as she watched him pull something from his pocket then drop down to one knee.

"I know we haven't really known each other that long, but it feels like we have. You wanted this gazebo for weddings, so I thought you and I could be the first to use it." He opened a little black box and lifted it so she could see the contents. A diamond ring winked back at her, embodying everything she'd wanted deep down but dared not hope for. "Audrey York, will you make me a very happy man and marry me?"

More tears welled in her eyes and spilled over. She covered her mouth to stifle a cry.

Brady's happy but nervous expression faded, replaced with worry. "I'm sorry. It's too soon."

He started to stand, but she placed her hands on his shoulders to keep him where he was. She shook her head. "No, it's not too soon. And yes, I will marry you."

Brady did stand then. Well, actually, he sprang to his feet and swept her off hers. She laughed as he spun her in a circle before placing her feet back on the step and kissing her until her head spun.

"You still sleepy?" he asked as he held her close.

"Who needs sleep?"

He placed his left arm behind her knees and swung

her into his arms. As he carried her toward the mill, she giggled.

"What's so funny?"

"Nothing." She ran her fingers over his biceps. "I was just thinking that all that manual labor comes in handy when you want to literally sweep a girl off her feet."

"Was that your ulterior motive for making me work so hard?"

She swatted his arm. "I didn't make you do anything."

He stepped inside the mill and headed for the stairs. "True. I would have done it all for free."

The way he said it, his words deep and husky, made her skin warm. She continued staring into his eyes as he carried her across the loft and set her on her feet at the foot of her bed. Without words, they started slowly undressing each other. With each button undone, each article of clothing dropped to the floor, the fact that she was going to spend the rest of her life with this man sank in a little more.

When all the clothes lay puddled at their feet, Brady lifted her again and lowered her onto the bed. She smiled as he slid in beside her.

"What's the smile for?" he asked.

"Because I'm happy. You make me happy."

He caressed her cheek. "The feeling's mutual." He lowered his lips to her mouth, then found his way to her neck, her ear, then blazed a trail of kisses to her breasts and stomach.

She ran her fingers through his hair and closed her eyes as all her nerve endings sparked to life.

Brady kissed his way back up the same trail. "You seem to be breathing a bit heavily," he teased as he reached her mouth again.

"And you're not breathing heavily enough." She grabbed him and pulled him down to her, letting all her desire flow into the kiss she gave him. She only broke the kiss and gasped when he joined with her. Her fingers gripped his muscled back as she met his movements with enthusiasm. How was it even possible to feel this good? This wonderfully complete?

They didn't have to be quiet, and they weren't. She no longer had to hold everything inside for fear the truth would ruin her life yet again. And that knowledge made their lovemaking even better. She found her release first, followed closely by Brady. Afterward, he cradled her close and she didn't think she'd ever felt so loved.

She noticed the light coming in the window for the first time. "You forgot to turn off the gazebo lights."

"Maybe I didn't forget." He nuzzled her ear. "Or maybe I had other things on my mind."

She laughed. "I thought when I pulled into the driveway tonight that I would be hitting this bed alone to sleep."

Brady shifted so he was looking down at her, his warm chest pressed against hers. "Sorry, I'm not going anywhere. But I figure you'll get that sleep." He lowered his mouth to hers and gave her a toe-curling kiss. "Eventually."

What was it she'd said out by the gazebo? Oh, yeah. Who needed sleep?

## Chapter Twelve

She wouldn't cry. Even though her mother should be here on her wedding day instead of on the other end of a phone line, Audrey refused to cry on this happiest of days. She didn't want to mess up her makeup or arrive next to Brady in a few minutes with red, puffy eyes.

"I wish you were here," she told her mom.

"I'm there in spirit, honey. I'm sure you are the most beautiful bride Tennessee has ever seen. Brady is a lucky man."

"I'm the lucky one. I don't think I've stopped smiling the entire two weeks since he proposed."

"I remember that feeling." Thomasina let out a sad sigh. "Your father would have loved walking you down the aisle. Is Nelson accompanying you?"

"No, I'm walking alone."

"Oh, sweetie."

"It's okay, really. It wouldn't feel right having someone other than you or Dad."

"I'm sorry."

Audrey made a scolding sound. "Now, what did we say about apologies?"

"That we'd said 'I'm sorry' enough to last a lifetime."

Quiet stretched between them for a moment. Audrey could hear the guests talking outside and her three new café employees, including magenta-haired Meg, downstairs getting things ready for the wedding reception to be followed by the café opening.

Word had not only gotten around about the new café but also about who she was. When she'd found out the latter, all her old fears had come back until Nelson had told her he'd made it clear at church that people weren't to judge her based on her mother's mistakes. And, well, once someone as respected as Nelson Witt made a proclamation in church, everyone seemed to fall in line.

"Audrey?"

"I'm here. Just daydreaming a little."

"Are you nervous?"

"Strangely, no. It all feels…right."

"I'm so happy for you. I can't wait to see the pictures."

"We're making a video for you, too, so you can feel like you were here."

"Oh, I'll be popular at movie night."

Audrey laughed. She was really proud of her mom. Not only was she beating a life-threatening disease, but she was trying to touch the lives of the women with whom she was incarcerated. She didn't call it a ministry, but in a way it was. A ministry of friendship and a shoulder to cry on and a willing ear to listen. Audrey had no doubt some of those women would lead better lives once they were released because of her mom's empathy.

A knock on the door drew Audrey's attention. "I think it's time for me to go."

"Enjoy this day to its absolute fullest. It'll be one of the happiest of your life."

"I will. I love you, Mom."

"I love you, too, sweetheart. Now go marry that handsome man."

Sophie poked her head in as Audrey hung up the phone. "You ready to make an honest man of my brother?"

Audrey laughed at her bridesmaid as she stood. "I suppose. I can't have his reputation in tatters." She took one last look at herself in the mirror, unable to believe the person looking back was her. She lifted her hand to the two pink rosebuds adorning the hair piled atop her head—one for each of her parents not here today. But even that tiny emptiness didn't dim how happy she was, like sunshine was bursting out of her.

"Okay, let's see if I can make it down the stairs without breaking my neck. I hear neck braces are so out in bridal wear this year."

Sophie had outdone herself, using all her bridal contacts to make the inside of the café and the gazebo look like a fairy tale, like it was a prince and princess getting married instead of a café owner and a construction worker. But as Audrey started down the stone path to the gazebo accompanied by gorgeous harp music, her eyes settled on Brady and she thought maybe Sophie had it right. She certainly felt like a princess, and Brady was definitely her prince.

Audrey looked across the dining room of the café from the kitchen's pickup window and felt a swell of pride. More than ever, she was convinced of karma's existence. For so long, it had seemed like her life was never going to be happy again. But today had been perfect—the weather, exchanging vows with Brady, how many of her new neighbors had shown up for the reception and promised to come often to sample the café's offerings.

She'd been stunned by the number of gifts and was convinced they were given because of Brady until people started talking to her as if they hadn't a clue she'd ever been touched by scandal. She and Brady had received everything from wineglasses to a homemade quilt to a brand-new Easy-Bake Oven from Sophie. Brady had turned a payback-is-hell look on his sister while she, Audrey, Nelson and Craig had nearly laughed themselves out of their chairs.

After the reception, the Willow Creek Café had officially opened for business and had been packed ever since. Sophie, who had taken a break from videotaping the café's opening at the end of the wedding tape, sat at a table with Nelson, Craig and Kelly. By the quick glances Kelly shot in Craig's direction, Audrey suspected the architecture intern had a serious case of the yearnings for Craig. Of course, Craig, being a clueless man, evidently hadn't noticed.

Audrey jumped when Brady wrapped his arms around her from behind and kissed her ear.

"Hello, Mrs. Witt."

A thrill went through her at the sound of her new name. She'd been Audrey York for so long that Audrey Witt was going to take some getting used to. But she did like the sound of it and all it represented.

"Hello, yourself. Thanks for helping tonight. We were busier than I anticipated."

Brady looked out into the dining room. "Seems to be slowing down a bit." He nuzzled her ear. "Why don't you leave the rest of the work to someone else so we can go have a proper wedding night."

She laughed as she turned in his arms. "I think perhaps we ought to have fewer people downstairs once the wedding night begins, don't you?"

"Then let's kick everyone out." He waggled his eyebrows at her.

She punched him playfully in the chest. "Yeah, that'd be really good for business."

"It'd be good for me."

"You are impossible." She gave him a quick kiss, then whispered, "We close at eight o'clock. We'll have a proper wedding night then."

"I can hardly wait."

That made two of them.

\* \* \* \* \*

"Chief Ranger Rossiter?" The sight of the woman who'd stepped inside Vance's office brought him to his feet. "I'm Rachel Darrow. Your secretary said I should come right in."

"Please," he said, walking around his desk to shake her hand. At a glance he estimated she was in her mid-twenties. Her feminine curves did wonders for the pale blue T-shirt and jeans she was wearing. "Ranger Jarvis informed me there's a young boy with you."

The unfriendly expression in her beautiful green eyes caught him off guard. "Yes," was her clipped reply. "When we arrived in Yosemite the ranger told me I couldn't go anywhere in the park until I talked to you first."

"That's right."

"Knowing you wanted this meeting to be private, he offered to show my nephew around Headquarters."

So this woman was the victim's sister.... "What's his name?"

"Nicky."

The boy who haunted Vance's dreams now had a name. "How old is he?"

"He turned six three weeks ago. Were you the man in charge when my brother and sister-in-law were killed?"

"Yes. To tell you I'm sorry for what happened couldn't begin to convey my feelings."

The woman's gaze didn't flicker. "I won't even try to describe mine. Just tell me one thing. Was their accident preventable?"

"Yes," he answered without hesitation.

"In other words, the people working under you fell asleep on your watch and two lives were snuffed out as a result."

Hearing it put like that, he had to set the record straight. "My staff had nothing to do with it. I, myself, could have prevented the loss of life."

Ms. Darrow's expression hardened. "So you admit culpability."

"Yes. I take full blame."

A look of pain crossed over her features. "You can just stand there and admit it?" Her cry echoed that of his own tortured soul.

"Yes." He sucked in his breath.

"I work for a cruise line. Aboard ship, it's the captain's responsibility to maintain rigid safety regulations. If a disaster like that had happened while he was in charge he would have been relieved of his command and never given another ship again."

Rachel Darrow couldn't know she was preaching to the converted. "If you've come to the park with the intention of bringing a lawsuit against me for negligence, maybe you should." It would only be what he deserved.

"Maybe I will."

In the next instant, she wheeled around and hurried out of his office. Vance could have gone after her, but it would cause a scene, something he was loath to do for a variety of reasons. In the first place, he needed to cool down before he approached her again.

The discovery of the Darrows' frozen bodies had affected every ranger in the park. A little boy had been orphaned—a boy whose aunt was all he had left.

\* \* \* \* \*

*Will Rachel allow Vance to explain—and will she let him into her heart?*
*Find out in*
*THE CHIEF RANGER*
*Available June 2009*
*from Harlequin® American Romance®.*

We'll be spotlighting a different series every month throughout 2009 to celebrate our 60th anniversary.

## Look for Harlequin® American Romance® in June!

Join us for a year-long celebration of the rugged American male! From cops to cowboys— Men Made in America has the hero you've been dreaming about!

Look for

# The Chief Ranger

### by Rebecca Winters, on sale in June!

# You're invited to join our Tell Harlequin Reader Panel!

By joining our new reader panel you will:

- Receive Harlequin® books—they are FREE and yours to keep with no obligation to purchase anything!
- Participate in fun online surveys
- Exchange opinions and ideas with women just like you
- Have a say in our new book ideas and help us publish the best in women's fiction

*In addition, you will have a chance to win great prizes and receive special gifts! See Web site for details. Some conditions apply. Space is limited.*

To join, visit us at
## www.TellHarlequin.com.

# REQUEST YOUR FREE BOOKS!

## 2 FREE NOVELS PLUS 2
## FREE GIFTS!

### Love, Home & Happiness!

**YES!** Please send me 2 FREE Harlequin® American Romance® novels and my 2 FREE gifts (gifts are worth about $10). After receiving them, if I don't wish to receive any more books, I can return the shipping statement marked "cancel." If I don't cancel, I will receive 4 brand-new novels every month and be billed just $4.24 per book in the U.S. or $4.99 per book in Canada.* That's a savings of close to 15% off the cover price! It's quite a bargain! Shipping and handling is just 50¢ per book. I understand that accepting the 2 free books and gifts places me under no obligation to buy anything. I can always return a shipment and cancel at any time. Even if I never buy another book from Harlequin, the two free books and gifts are mine to keep forever.

154 HDN EYSE  354 HDN EYSQ

| | |
|---|---|
| Name | (PLEASE PRINT) |
| Address | Apt. # |
| City | State/Prov. | Zip/Postal Code |

Signature (if under 18, a parent or guardian must sign)

### Mail to the **Harlequin Reader Service:**
**IN U.S.A.:** P.O. Box 1867, Buffalo, NY 14240-1867
**IN CANADA:** P.O. Box 609, Fort Erie, Ontario L2A 5X3

Not valid to current subscribers of Harlequin® American Romance® books.

**Want to try two free books from another line?**
**Call 1-800-873-8635 or visit www.morefreebooks.com.**

* Terms and prices subject to change without notice. Prices do not include applicable taxes. N.Y. residents add applicable sales tax. Canadian residents will be charged applicable provincial taxes and GST. Offer not valid in Quebec. This offer is limited to one order per household. All orders subject to approval. Credit or debit balances in a customer's account(s) may be offset by any other outstanding balance owed by or to the customer. Please allow 4 to 6 weeks for delivery. Offer available while quantities last.

**Your Privacy:** Harlequin is committed to protecting your privacy. Our Privacy Policy is available online at www.eHarlequin.com or upon request from the Reader Service. From time to time we make our lists of customers available to reputable third parties who may have a product or service of interest to you. If you would prefer we not share your name and address, please check here. □

HAR09R

# HARLEQUIN® *Romance*®

## *Escape Around the World*
### *Dream destinations, whirlwind weddings!*

# *Honeymoon with the Boss*
### by
# JESSICA HART

Top tycoon Tom Maddison is used to calling the shots—until his convenient marriage falls through. But rather than waste his honeymoon, he'll take his boardroom to the beach and bring his oh-so-sensible secretary Imogen on a tropical business trip! But will Tom finally see the sexy woman that prudent Imogen truly is?

*Available in June wherever books are sold.*

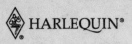

# HARLEQUIN®

## *American ★ Romance*®

## COMING NEXT MONTH
### Available June 9, 2009

**#1261 THE CHIEF RANGER by Rebecca Winters**
*Men Made in America*
As the chief ranger of Yosemite National Park, Vance Rossiter isn't surprised to be confronted by Rachel Darrow, a woman whose brother perished on El Capitan during a blizzard. It happened on his watch, he's to blame—and he'll do anything to make things right. Including taking Nicky, Rachel's orphaned nephew, under his wing. And educating Rachel about what really happened that fateful day…

**#1262 MOMMY FOR HIRE by Cathy Gillen Thacker**
Why Grady McCabe needs to buy a wife is a mystery to Alexis Graham. The attractive and wealthy developer isn't looking for love—only a mother for his little girl. Alexis can't imagine marrying for anything *but* love. Then when the matchmaking widow tries to change a certain Texan's mind, he starts to relent… and fall for *her*!
*A special, bonus story from The McCabes of Texas miniseries!*

**#1263 THE TEXAS TWINS by Tina Leonard**
When New York billionaire John Carruth came to No Chance, Texas, to save their rodeo from bankruptcy, he had no idea he'd be meeting his twin brother. Jake Fitzgerald, champion bull rider, didn't know he had another half. John may be kin, but he's still a stranger in these parts. It's a showdown between two rivals, to see which brother will win the woman of his dreams—and be the town's savior!
The Billionaire *and* The Bull Rider—*2 stories in 1!*

**#1264 WAITING FOR BABY by Cathy McDavid**
*Baby To Be*
Lilly Russo is thrilled—and terrified—to be pregnant. It's a bit of a shock that her brief affair with the owner of Bear Creek Ranch, Jake Tucker, led to a new life growing inside her. She's worried about being a mom, but she's even more concerned about Jake, already a busy single father of three girls. Can their relationship grow from a fling into love—considering there's a baby at stake?

www.eHarlequin.com

HARCNMBPA0509